EIGHT KEYS TO EDEN

EIGHT KEYS
TO EDEN
by
Mark Clifton

WILDSIDE PRESS

www.wildsidepress.com

All of the characters in this book
are fictitious, and any resemblance
to actual persons, living or dead,
is purely coincidental.

To

Charles Steinberg

who made writing possible for me

EIGHT KEYS TO EDEN

SEVEN DOORS TO SEVEN ROOMS OF THOUGHT

1 Accept the statement of Eminent Authority without basis, without question.

2 Disagree with the statement without basis, out of general contrariness.

3 Perhaps the statement is true, but what if it isn't? How then to account for the phenomenon?

4 How much of the statement rationalizes to suit man's purpose that he and his shall be ascendant at the center of things?

5 What if the minor should become major, the recessive dominant, the obscure prevalent?

6 What if the statement were reversible, that which is considered effect is really cause?

7 What if the natural law perceived in one field also operates unperceived in all other phases of science. What if there be only one natural law manifesting itself, as yet, to us in many facets because we cannot apperceive the whole, of which we have gained only the most elementary glimpses, with which we can cope only at the crudest level?

And are those still other doors, yet undefined, on down the corridor?

1

One minute after the regular report call from the planet Eden was overdue, the communications operator summoned his supervisor. His finger hesitated over the key reluctantly, then he gritted his teeth and pressed it down. The supervisor came boiling out of his cubicle, half-running down the long aisle between the forty operators hunched over their panels.

"What is it? What is it?" he quarreled, even before he came to a stop.

"Eden's due. Overdue." The operator tried to make it laconic, but it came out sullen.

The supervisor rubbed his forehead with his knuckles and punched irritably at some buttons on an astrocalculator. An up-to-the-second star map lit up the big screen at the end of the room. He didn't expect there to be any occlusions to interfere with the communications channel. The astrophysicists didn't set up reporting schedules to include such blunders. But he had to check.

There weren't.

He heaved a sigh of exasperation. Trouble always had to come on his shift, never anybody else's.

"Lazy colonists probably neglecting to check in on time," he rationalized cynically to the operator. He rubbed his long nose and hoped the operator would agree that's all it was.

The operator looked skeptical instead.

Eden was still under the first five-year tests. Five-year experimental colonists were arrogant, they were zany, they were a lot of things, some unprintable, which qualified them for being test colonizers and nothing else apparently. They were almost as much of a problem as the Extrapolators.

But they weren't lazy. They didn't forget.

"Some fool ship captain has probably messed up communications by inserting a jump band of his own." The supervisor hopefully tried out another idea. Even to him it sounded weak. A jump band didn't last more than an instant, and no ship captain would risk his license by using the E frequency, anyway.

He looked hopefully down the long room at the bent heads of the other operators at their panels. None was signaling an emergency to draw him away from this; give him an excuse to leave in the hope the problem would have solved itself by the time he could get back to it. He chewed on a knuckle and stared angrily at the operator who was sitting back, relaxed, looking at him, waiting.

"You sure you're tuned to the right frequency for Eden?" the supervisor asked irritably. "You sure your equipment is working?"

The operator pulled a wry mouth, shrugged, and didn't bother to answer with more than a nod. He allowed a slight expression of contempt for supervisors who asked silly questions to show. He caught the surreptitious wink of the operator at the next panel, behind the supervisor's back. The disturbance was beginning to attract attention. In response to the wink he pulled the dogged expression of the unjustly nagged employee over his features.

"Well, why don't you give Eden an alert, then!" the supervisor muttered savagely. "Blast them out of their seats. Make 'em get off their—their pants out there!"

The operator showed an expression which plainly said it was about time, and reached over to press down the emergency key. He held it down. Eleven light-years away, if one had to depend upon impossibly slow three-dimensional space time, a siren which could be heard for ten miles in Eden's atmosphere should be blaring.

The supervisor stood and watched while he transferred the gnawing at his knuckles to his fingernails.

He waited, with apprehensive satisfaction, for some angry colonist to come through and scream at them to turn off that unprintable-phrases siren. He braced himself and worked up some choice phrases of his own to scream back at the colonist for neglecting his duty—getting Extrapolation Headquarters here on Earth all worked up over nothing. He wondered if he dared threaten to send an Extrapolator out there to check them over.

He decided the threat would have no punch. An E would pay no attention to his recommendation. He knew it, and the colonist would know it too.

He began to wonder what excuse the colonist would have.

"Just wanted to see if you home-office boys were on your toes," the insolent colonist would drawl. Probably something like that.

He hoped the right words wouldn't fail him.

But there was no response to the siren.

"Lock the key down," he told the operator. "Keep it blasting until they wake up."

He looked down the room and saw that a couple of the near operators were now frankly listening.

"Get on with your work," he said loudly. "Pay attention to what you're recording."

It was enough to cause several more heads to raise.

"Now, now, now!" he chattered to the room at large. "This is nothing to concern the rest of you. Just a delayed report, that's all. Haven't you ever heard of a delayed report before?"

He shouldn't have asked that, because of course they had. It was like asking a mountain climber if he had ever felt a taut rope over the razor edge of a precipice suddenly go slack.

"But there's nothing any of you can do," he said. He tried to cover the plaintive note by adding, "And if you louse up your own messages . . ." But he had threatened them so often that there was no longer any menace.

He spent the next ten minutes hauling out the logs of Eden to see if they'd ever been tardy before. The logs covered two and a fraction years, two years and four months. The midgit-idgit scanner didn't pick up a single symbol to show that Eden had been even two seconds off schedule. The first year daily, the second year weekly, and now monthly. There wasn't a single hiccough from the machine to kick out an Extrapolator's signal to watch for anything unusual.

Eden heretofore had presented about as much of an *outré* problem as an Iowa cornfield.

"You're really sure your equipment is working?" he asked again as he came back to stand behind the operator's chair. "They haven't answered yet."

The operator shrugged again. It was pretty obvious the colonists hadn't answered. And what should he do about it? Go out there personally and shake his finger at them—naughty, naughty?

"Well why don't you bounce a beam on the planet's surface, to see?" the supervisor grumbled. "I want to see an echo. I want to see for myself that you haven't let your equipment go sour. Or maybe there's a space hurricane between here and there. Or maybe a booster has blown. Or maybe some star has exploded and warped things. Maybe. . . . Well, bounce it, man. Bounce it! What are you waiting for?"

"Okay, okay!" the operator grumbled back. "I was waiting for you to give the order." He grimaced at the operator behind the supervisor. "I can't just go bouncing beams on planets if I happen to be in the mood."

"Now, now. Now, now. No insubordination, if you please," the supervisor cautioned.

Together they waited, in growing dread, for the automatic relays strung out through space to take hold, automatically calculating the route, set up the required space-jump bands. It was called instantaneous communication, but that was only relative. It took time.

The supervisor was frowning deeply now. He hated to report to the sector chief that an emergency had come up which he couldn't handle. He hated the thought of Extrapolators poking around in his department, upsetting the routines, asking questions he'd already asked. He hated the forethought of the admiration he'd see in the eyes of his operators when an E walked into the room, the eagerness with which they'd respond to questions, the thrill of merely being in the same room.

He hated the operators, in advance, for giving freely of admiration to an E that they withheld from him. He allowed himself the momentary secret luxury of hating all Extrapolators. Once upon a time, when he was a kid, he had dreamed of becoming an E. What kid hadn't? He'd gone farther than the wish. He'd tried. And had been rebuffed.

"Clinging to established scientific beliefs," the tester had told him with the inherent, inescapable superiority of a man trying to be kind to a lesser intelligence, "is like being afraid to jump off a precipice in full confidence that you'll think of something to save yourself before you hit bottom."

It might or might not have been figurative, but he had allowed himself the pleasure of wishing the tester would try it.

"To accept what Eminent Authority says as true," the tester had continued kindly, "wouldn't even qualify you for being a scientist. Although," he added hopefully, "this would not bar you from an excellent career in engineering."

It was a bitter memory of failure. For if you disbelieved what science said was true, where were you? And if it might not be true, why was it said? Even now he shuddered at the chaos he would have to face, live with. No certainties on which to stand.

He washed the memory out of his thought, and concentrated on the flashing pips that chased themselves over the operator's screen. There was nothing wrong with the equipment. Nothing wrong with the communication channels between Eden and Earth.

"Blasted colonists," the supervisor muttered. "Instead of a beam on their planet, I'd like to bounce a rock on their heads. I'll bet they've let all the sets at their end get out of order."

He knew it was a foolish statement, even if the operator's face hadn't told him so. Any emergency colonist, man or woman—and there were fifty of them on Eden—could build a communicator. That was regulation.

"You sure there haven't been any emergency calls from them?" he asked the operator with sudden suspicion. "You're not covering up some neglect in not notifying me? If you're covering up, you'd better tell me now. I'll find out. It'll all come out in the investigation, and. . . ."

The operator turned around and looked at him levelly. He looked him over, with open contempt, from bald head to splayed feet. Then he coolly turned his back. There was a limit to just how much a man could stand, even to hold a job at E Headquarters.

It was about time the supervisor got somebody with brains onto the job. The sector chief should be called immediately. Supervisors were supposed to have enough brains to think of something so obvious as that. That much brains at least.

2

The first reaction of the sector chief to the dreaded words "delayed report" was a shocked negation, an illusory belief that it couldn't happen to him.

To the intense annoyance of the communications supervisor, his first act was to rush down to communications and go through all the routines for rousing the colonists the supervisor had tried. His worry was mounting so rapidly that he hardly noticed the resigned expression of the operator who knew he would have to go through all these useless motions again and again before it was all over, and somebody did something.

"Well," the chief said to the supervisor. "It's my problem now." He sighed, and unconsciously squared his shoulders.

"Yes, Chief Hayes," the supervisor agreed quickly. Perhaps too quickly, with too much relief? "Well, that is, I mean . . ." his voice trailed off. After all, it was.

"You understand my check of your routines was no reflection on you or your department," Hayes said diplomatically. "It's a heavy responsibility to alert E.H.Q., pull the scientists off who knows what delicate, critical work—maybe even hope to get the attention of an E—all that. I had to make sure, you know."

"Of course, Chief Hayes," the supervisor said, and relaxed some of his resentment. "Serious matter," he chattered. "Disgrace if an

E, without half trying, put his finger on our oversight. We all understand that." He tried to include the nearby operators, his boys, in his eager agreement, but they were all busy showing how intensely they had to concentrate on their work.

"That's probably all it is—an oversight," Hayes said with unconvincing reassurance; then, at the hurt look on the supervisor's face, added, "Beyond our control here, of course. Something it would take at least a scientist to spot, something we couldn't be expected . . . What I mean is, we shouldn't get alarmed until we know, for sure. And—ah—keep it confidential."

"Of course, Chief Hayes," the supervisor said in a near whisper. He looked meaningfully around at the room of operators, but did manage not to put his finger to his lips. Those who were observing out of the corners of their eyes were grateful for at least that.

On his way back to his own office Chief William Hayes reflected that the bit about keeping it confidential was on the corny side. Within fifteen minutes he'd start spreading it all over E.H.Q., himself. Every scientist, every lab assistant would know it. Every clerk, every janitor would know it. E.H.Q. would have to work full blast all night long, and some of the lesser personnel had homes down in Yellow Sands at the foot of the mountain.

These would be calling their husbands and wives, telling them not to fix dinner, not to worry if they didn't come home all night. No matter how guarded, the news would leak out, the word spread, and the newscast reporters would pick it up for the delectation of the public. Eden colony cut off from communication. Nobody knows . . . Wonder . . . Fear . . . Delicious . . . Exciting. . . .

Or was this the kind of thinking that had kept him from qualifying as an E? What was it the examiner had asked? "Mr. Hayes, why do you feel it is all right for you to view, to read, to know—but that others should be protected from seeing, reading, knowing? What are these sterling qualities you have that make it all right for you to censor what would not be right for others?"

He abruptly brought his mind back to the present. Perhaps he'd first better prepare a news statement before he did anything else, something noncommittal, reassuring. No point in getting the populace stirred up.

As he sat down behind his desk, a big man in a brown suit, natural iron-gray hair, a calm and administrative face, he began to realize that for the next twenty-four hours, at least, he would be in the spotlight. Well, he'd give a good account of himself. Demonstrate that he had an executive capacity beyond the needs of his present job. More than a mere requisition signer, interoffice memo initialer.

For one thing the scientists would give him trouble. If he had been deeply hurt that they thought he couldn't open up his mind enough to become an E, what about scientists whose limits were reached still farther along? He must remember to keep his temper, use persuasion, maybe kid them a little. The blasted experts were almost as bad as E's—worse, in a way, because the E didn't have to remind anybody of his dignity, or how important the work was he was doing.

But then, you never asked an E to drop what he was doing, and listen. You never asked an E to do anything. He either noticed and was interested, or he didn't notice, or wasn't interested.

But nobody ever told an E that he must apply himself to a problem. Once a man became a full-fledged Extrapolator he was outside all law, all frameworks, all duty, all social mores. That was the essence of E science, that any requirement outside of his own making didn't exist. It had to be that way. That kind of mind could not tolerate barriers, but spent itself constantly in destroying them. Erect barriers of triviality, and it would waste its substance upon trivial matters. The only answer was to remove all possible barriers for the E, lest immersion in something trivial prevent that mind from seeking out a barrier to knowledge, a problem of significance.

But the scientists! Hayes sighed. If only the scientists wouldn't keep thinking they were cut from the same cloth as the E. They had to have restrictions, organization imposed upon them. Yes indeed!

They'd grumble at being taken away from their work to assemble a review of all the known facts about Eden—a dead issue as far as their own work was concerned, for Eden had been assayed and filed away as solved. They'd moan and groan about having to drag up the facts that had been analyzed and settled long ago.

He saw himself compared with the producer of a show, and theatrical performers didn't come any more temperamental than scientists. He'd be hearing about how much of their time he'd wasted for months to come. Every time any administrator asked why they hadn't produced whatever it was they were working on, it would be because Chief Hayes had interrupted them at the most crucial moment and they'd had to begin all over again.

Oh, they'd drag their heels, all right, and he'd have to remind them, tactfully, that their prime duty was to serve the Extrapolators; that they were employed here only because someday, in some co-ordinate system, somebody might be able to supply a key fact that some E might want to know.

They'd ask him, slyly, what guarantee he had that any E would be listening if they did produce a review of the Eden complex, knowing he could give no such guarantee.

They'd drag their heels because, deep down, they carried a basic resentment against the E—because, experts though they were, each of them, somewhere along the line, had learned the bitter limits in his mind that prevented him from going on to become an E.

They'd drag their heels because the E's, each blasted one of them, would regard the absolutely true facts proved beyond question by science with an attitude of skepticism, temporarily accepting the uncontestably immutable as only provisional, and probably quite wrong.

Oh, they'd grumble, and they'd drag their heels at first; but they would get into it. They'd get into it, not because the sector chief had babied them along, kidded them, coaxed them, but because, as surely as his name was Bill Hayes, some unprintable E would ask a question for which they had no answer. Or even worse, some question that made no sense, but left the scientist feeling that perhaps it should have!

That was the E brand of thinking which gave everybody trouble —and without which man could never have gone on creeping outward and outward among the stars. Every new planet, or subplanet, or sun or blasted asteroid seemed to call for some revision of known laws. Sometimes an entirely new co-ordinate system had to be resolved. Oh, science was easy, a veritable snap, while man crawled around on the muddy bottom of his ocean of air and concluded that throughout all the universe things must conform to his then notion of what they must be. As ignorant as a damned halibut must be of the works and thoughts of man.

And often the E was unable to resolve the co-ordinate system —which was simply a euphemistic way of saying that he didn't come back. And without him, man could go no farther. An E, therefore, was the rarest and most valuable piece of property in the universe. Whatever else man might be, he will go to any lengths to protect the value of his property.

All right, Bill, perhaps a part of that is true. But give the scientists their full due. They'd work with a will once they grew aware of the need of it, because they were just as concerned as anybody else with what might have happened to those colonists.

But first they would argue.

His secretary interrupted his thought by coming in from her own office. She had an inch-thick stack of midgit-idgit cards in her hand.

"Here's that batch of scientists who worked on the original Eden survey," she said.

"So many?" Hayes asked ruefully. "Maybe I'd better send an all-points bulletin."

"You're the boss," she said easily. "But if I know scientists, they don't read bulletins."

"Yeah, sure," he agreed. "You made sure this is everybody? Nobody is slighted? They'll scream like stuck pigs when I ask them, but they'll be even worse if I slight anybody by not asking."

"Double checked with Personnel's own midgit-idgit," she replied. "The machine says if anybody is left out, it's not its fault, that it would only be because we stupid humans forgot to inform it in the first place."

"Sometimes I think that machine complains more than people do," he answered. "Certainly it is a lot more insolent."

"Gets more work done, though," she said comfortably. "You want anything more?"

"Not right now."

"Buzz if you do. The idgit is working out the supply list for that new exploration ship, and it wants service, too," she reminded him. "It's worse than you are," she added.

He looked up at her familiarity with a twinkle.

"It can't fire you," he said softly.

"Oh?" she asked. "You think not? Just let me feed it a few wrong data and watch what happens to your li'l ol' lovin' secretary." She winked at him, laughed, and went back to her office.

Sector Chief Hayes sighed, and pulled the stack of cards toward him. First he must sort them out according to protocol because his diplomacy wouldn't be worth the breath used in it if he called the wrong man first. At a glance he saw that the idgit had already sorted them correctly according to status.

"If you're so smart," he muttered to the absent machine, "why didn't you call them too?"

He picked up the first card, and dialed the man's intercom number. It would be like opening the lid of Pandora's box. . . .

At that instant the red light of the E intercom flashed on. Hayes dropped the ordinary key back into its slot, and pushed the E key to open. He did not recognize the voice that came through.

"How soon," the voice asked, "will we be able to get into this Eden matter?"

"I'm setting it up now," he said quickly. "By tomorrow morning, surely. That is, if we haven't solved it ourselves. Something minor that wouldn't require an E."

"Morning will be fine. Two, possibly three Seniors will be available."

The red light flashed off, showing the connection had been broken. He sat back in his chair, suddenly conscious that his forehead was wet with sweat, that his shirt was sticking to his body. Not conscious that he was grinning joyfully.

Now let those pesty scientists challenge him with the question of whether any E's would be listening to their review. Two of 'em. Maybe three. Besides, of course, all the Juniors, the apprentices, the students.

He dialed the first scientist again. But this time he didn't mind it being Pandora's box. It was a terrible thing for a man to realize he could never be an E. The scientists had to take it out on somebody. He understood.

"Hello, Dr. Mille," he said cordially in answer to a gruff grunt. "This is Bill Hayes, of Sector Administration."

"All right! All right!" the voice answered testily. "What is it now?"

3

In the early dawn, out at the hangar, away from the main E buildings and the endless discussions going on inside them, Thomas R. Lynwood moved methodically through his preflight inspection.

Speculative thinking was none of his concern. His job was to pilot an E wherever he might want to go, and bring him back again—if possible. To Lynwood reality was a physical thing—the feel of controls beneath his broad, square hands; the hum of machinery responsive to his will. He liked mathematics not for its own sake but because it best described the substance of things, the weight, the size, the properties of things, how they behaved. He was too intelligent not to realize mathematics could also communicate speculative unrealities, but he was content to wait until the theorists had turned such equations into machines, controls, forces before he got excited.

He was one who, even in childhood, had never wanted to be an E. He didn't want to be one now. Somebody had once told him in Personnel that was why he was a favorite pilot of the E's, but he discounted that. They didn't try to tell him how to run his ship—well, most of them didn't—and he didn't try to tell them how to solve their problems.

The men around the hangar had another version of why the E's liked him to pilot them around—he was lucky. Somehow he always managed to come back, and bring the E with him. Well, sure. He didn't want to get stuck somewhere, wind up in a gulio's gullet, gassed by an atmosphere that turned from oxygen-nitrogen into pure methane without warning or reason, and against all known chemical laws, or whiffed out in the lash of a dead star suddenly gone nova.

But sometimes a pilot couldn't help himself. These E's would fiddle around in places where human beings shouldn't have gone. Most of the time they weren't allowed even one mistake. He was lucky, sure, but part of it might be because he'd never been sent out with the wrong E.

There could be a first time. Luck ran out if you kept piling your bets higher and higher. But until then . . .

He was square-jawed, a freckled man with red hair. Contrary to superstition, he didn't have a fiery temper. He was forty and had already built up a seniority of twenty years in deep space. He was captain of his ship and wanted nothing more. Sure, it was only a three-man crew—himself, a flight engineer, an astro-navigator. But it was an E ship, which meant that he outranked even the captains of the great luxury liners.

There was a time when the realization caused him to strut a little, but he'd got over it. He was single, had no ties, wanted none. He had a good job which he took seriously, was doing significant work which he also took seriously, was paid premium wages even for a space captain, which didn't matter except in terms of recognition. He didn't mind going anywhere in the known universe, or how long he would be away. He hoped he would get back someday, but he wasn't fanatic about it.

In a routine so well-practiced that it had become ritual, he checked over the cruiser point by point. Of course the maintenance men had checked each item when they had, after his last trip, dismantled, cleaned, oiled, polished, tested, and reassembled one part after another. Then maintenance supervisors had checked over the ship with a gimlet-eyed attitude of hoping to find some flaw, just one tiny flub, so they could turn some luckless mechanic inside out. The Inspection Department, traditionally an enemy of Maintenance, took over from there and inspected every part as if it had been slapped together by a bunch of army goof-offs who knew that pilots were expendable in peace or war and, unconsciously at least, aided in expending them.

Both departments had certified, with formal preflight papers, that the ship was in readiness for deep space. But Lynwood considered such papers as so much garbage, and went over the entire ship himself. This might have had something to do with his so-called luck.

He wondered if Frank and Louie had checked into the ship this morning. Probably had; last night's outing wasn't much to hang over about. A steak at the Eagle Cafe down in Yellow Sands, a couple of drinks at Smitty's, a game of pool at Smiley's, a few dances at the Stars and Moons. Big night out for his crew before they left for deep space. Yellow Sands was strictly for young families, where bright-boy hubby worked up on the hill at E.H.Q., and wifey raised super-bright kids who already considered Dad to be behind the times. Their idea of sin in that town was to snub the wrong matron at a cocktail party; or not snub, as the case might be. Not that it mattered much, neither Frank nor Louie was dedicated to hell-raising.

When he at last opened the door to the generator room, he saw his flight engineer, Frank Norton, had a couple of student E's on his hands.

It was one of the nuisances of being stationed here at E.H.Q. that you'd have swarms of these super-bright youngsters hanging around, asking questions, disputing your answers, arguing with each other, and, if you didn't watch them carefully, taking things apart and putting them back together in different hookups to see what would happen.

The first thing these kids were taught was to disregard everything everybody had ever said; to start out from scratch as if nobody had ever had the sense to think about the problem before; to doubt most of all the opinions of experts, for, obviously, if the experts were right then there would be no problem. Most of them didn't have to be taught it, they seemed to have been born with it. Time was you batted a young smart aleck down, told him to go get dry behind the ears before he shot off his mouth. But not these days. These days you looked at him hopefully, and crossed your fingers. He might grow up to be an E.

Tom wondered what it would be like to doubt the realities, the very machinery under his hands, to assume that although it had always worked it might not work this time. He could not conceive that state of mind, or how a man could live in it without going insane. Everytime he saw these tortured kids saying, "Well, maybe, but what if . . ." he was glad to be nothing more than a ship captain who knew his machinery was exactly what it was supposed to be and nothing else.

But, in a way, it was nice for the lads too. After thousands of years of man's almost rabid determination to destroy the brightest and best of his young, the world had finally found a place for the bright boy.

This morning, probably because of the early dawn hour, there were only two of them in the generator room. As expected, they were arguing over the space-jump band. Frank was standing over to one side, observing but not participating. His cap was pushed back on his blond head, his big face expressionless. It was common gossip throughout flight crews everywhere that Frank, blindfolded, could take a cruiser apart and put it back together without missing a motion.

"The jump band is founded on the basic of the Moebius strip," one student E was saying heatedly. "This little gadget sends out a field in the shape of such a strip, a band with a half twist before rejoined. Its width is as variable as we need it, up to a light year."

"Only it hasn't any width at all," the other student argued. "That's the whole point. The Moebius strip has only one edge, so it can't have width. We enter that edge, go through a line that doesn't exist, and come out a light-year away, without taking any longer than the time to pass a point."

"But that's *what* happens, not *how*," the other shouted angrily. "Everybody knows *what* happens. Tell me *how* and maybe I'll listen."

Tom caught his flight engineer's eye and signaled with his head that it might be a good idea to get rid of the students. Any other time it would be all right, a part of their stand-by job, but they'd got word last night to have the ship in readiness from six o'clock on. They might have to wait all day, but then again, some E might get an idea and want to go shooting out to Eden right off.

Frank caught the signal, grinned, and began to herd the two students toward the door. They were in such heated argument now, accusing one another of parrot repetition instead of thinking for himself, that they didn't realize that they were being nudged out of the ship, down its ramp, and out on the field.

"Don't think it hasn't been educational, and all," Frank murmured to them as he got them off the ramp. "You get the how of it figured out, you let me know."

The two looked at him as if he might be an interesting phenomenon, decided he wasn't, and wandered away, back toward the school dormitories, still arguing.

"Sometimes I think a quiet milk run out to Saturn would have its brighter side," Frank muttered to Tom when he came back inside the ship. Tom grinned at him in wordless understanding.

There was no tension between them. They had worked together so long that they had got over all the attraction-repulsion conflicts which operate far beneath the surface mind to cause likes and dislikes. Now they accepted one another in the way a man accepts his own hands—proud of them when they do something with extra skill, making allowances when they fumble; but never considering doing without them.

"Wonder who the E will be this time?" Frank asked, without too much concern. It didn't really matter. An E was an E, for better or for worse.

"Haven't heard," Tom answered. "Probably not decided yet. If the Senior E's think it isn't much of a problem, they might send a Junior. Or if they don't want to be bothered, they might send a Junior who's up for his solo problem."

"Whoever, or whatever, I'm sure it will be interesting," Frank commented with a grin. Tom returned the grin. There wasn't any malice in it, nor any of the basic enmity and destructiveness of the stupid toward the bright, just a recognition that an E was an E. They had a vast respect for an E, but you couldn't get around it that some of them were—well, maybe eccentric was the word.

"I hear there's trouble on that planet we're going to—Eden, isn't it?" Frank commented.

"You think we'd be hauling an E out there if there weren't?" Tom countered wryly.

They continued to check over each item in the generator room, their flying fingers making sharp contrast to their slow, idle conversation. They gave the room extra care this time because there had been some quick-fingered students around who just might have got it into their heads to improve the machinery. Satisfied at last that there had been no subtle meddling, they snapped the cowl of the generator back into position. They took one more sharp look around, then walked, single file, up the narrow passage to the control room. Louie LeBeau was sitting in the astro-navigator's seat, checking over his star charts and instruments. He glanced up at them as they came level with his cubicle. He was the third man of the team, as used to them as they were to him.

"Fourteen hop adjustments to get us past Pluto and out of the heavy traffic," he grumbled sourly. His round face and liquid brown eyes were perpetually disgusted. "They keep saying over at Traffic that they're going to provide a freeway out of the solar system so we can take it in one hop, but they don't do it. Wonder when we'll ever go modern, start doing things scientific?"

They paid no attention to his grumbling. That was just Louie.

"Then how many hops to Eden, after Pluto?" Tom asked.

"I figure twenty," Louie answered. "Can't take full light-year leaps every time. There's stuff in the way. There's always stuff in the way to louse up a good flight plan. Universe is too crowded. There'll be no trouble getting *to* Eden, no trouble *getting* there. Make it in about fourteen hours. Fourteen hours to go eleven lousy little light-years. Fourteen hours I got to work in one stretch. Wait'll the union agent hears you're working me fourteen hours without a relief. And are you letting me get my rest now, so I can work fourteen hours? Or are you stopping me from resting with a lot of questions?"

"But you think there may be trouble *after* we get to Eden?" Tom asked.

Louie looked at him. There was no fear in the soft, brown eyes; just an enormous indignation that life should always treat him so dirty.

"Don't you?" he asked.

4

Calvin Gray, Junior Extrapolator, stood nude before his bathroom mirror and played a no-beard light over his chin and thin cheeks. That should take care of the beard problem for the next six months or so. He leaned forward and examined the fine lines beginning to appear at the corners of his eyes. Well, that was one of the signs he'd reached the thirty mark. One couldn't stay forever at the peak of youth—not yet, anyway. Perhaps he should think about that sometime.

Trouble was, there was always something more urgent. . . .

He became conscious that Linda was standing in the bathroom door watching him. He hadn't heard her get out of bed.

"You used the no-beard just last month, Cal," she said. There was a questioning note in her voice.

"Want to keep handsome," he said lightly. "Never know when I might have to run out to some other world. Wouldn't want one of my other wives to catch me with stubble on my face."

It was a stale joke, a childish one, but it served to introduce the topic foremost in his mind.

"This Eden problem. I can't plan on it, but I hope it's my solo to qualify me for my big E. I'm due, you know."

Linda chose to avoid coming directly to grips with it.

"Yehudi is already at the door," she said, and made a face of exasperation. "Someday I'm going to turn off the gadget that signals the orderly room the minute you get out of bed, so I can have you all to myself."

"It's better if you get used to him," Cal cautioned. "Turn off the signal and that turns on an alarm. Instead of one Yehudi, you'd have twenty rushing in to see what was wrong."

"Well, it seems to me a grown man ought to be able to take his morning shower without an observer standing by to see that he doesn't drown himself or swallow the soap," she commented with a touch of acid.

"Get used to it, woman," he commanded. "There's only one observer now. When—if I get my senior rating, there'll be three."

She didn't say anything. Instead she stepped over to him, pressed her nude body against his, and tenderly nuzzled his arm.

"Maybe if we go back to bed, he'll go away," she said, and glittered her eyes at him wickedly.

"He won't, but it's a good idea," Cal grinned at her.

"You could tell him to go away," she whispered with a little pout.

She was fighting. She was fighting with the only weapon she had to hold him, to keep him from going away, to face an unknown. He knew it, and the bitterness in her eyes, back of her teasing, showed she knew he knew it.

He took her tenderly in his arms, held her close to him, stroked her hair, kissed her mouth. She pulled her face away, buried it in his chest. He felt her sobbing.

He picked her up, lightly, carried her back into the bedroom, laid her gently on the bed, and, oblivious to the attendant who stood expressionless inside the door, knelt down beside the bed and held her head in his arms.

"Don't fight it," he said softly. "It isn't the first time a man has had to go."

"It's the first time it ever happened to me," she sobbed. "You knew when you married me. . . . You agreed. . . ."

"It was easy to agree, then. There was the glamor of being

known as the wife of an E. Now that doesn't matter. There's just you, and the thought of losing you, never seeing you again."

"I haven't gone yet," he reminded her. "I don't know that I'll get the job. There are three Seniors at base right now. One of them might want it. Even if I do get the problem, who says I won't be back? You take old McGinnis. He's eighty if he's a day. He's been an E for nigh on to fifty years. He's still around, you'll notice."

She was quieter now. She lay, looking at him, drinking in his dark hair, blue eyes, handsome face, the shape of his intelligent head, the slope of his neck and shoulders, the tapering waist, all the masculine grace and beauty. She pressed her closed fist into her mouth. All the beauty she might never see again, feel enfolded around her, enfold with herself.

"I'm a little fool," she said through clenched teeth. "Of course you'll be back. And you'd better make it quick, or I'll come after you."

He kissed her, rumpled her short hair, straightened her crumpled body on the bed, pulled the sheet over her.

"Why don't you go back to sleep," he suggested. "Rest. I'll have breakfast in the E club room. That's where we'll be watching the Eden briefing. Sleep. Sleep all morning."

Gently he closed her eyes with the tip of his forefinger. Gently he kissed her once more. This time she didn't cling to him, try to hold him.

He tucked the sheet in around her throat. Dutifully, she kept her eyes closed. He stood up then, and signaled the orderly.

"I'll take my shower now," he said.

The orderly didn't speak, just followed him into the bathroom to stand in the doorway and watch him through the shower glass. He was rigidly obeying the cardinal rule of E.H.Q.

Unless his life is in danger, never interrupt the thinking of an E. The whole course of man's destiny in the universe may depend on it.

How much of the future of the universe depended upon his

not interrupting the scene he had just witnessed wasn't for him to say. He sighed. He thought of his own wife—shrewish, fat, coarse, always complaining. He wondered what she would do if he picked her up, carried her to bed, closed her eyes with his fingers. For once, he'd bet, she'd be speechless.

He must try it sometime. But first, she'd have to lose about fifty pounds.

When Cal got to the E club room two Seniors were already there—McGinnis and Wong. He thought their greeting was a shade more cordial, a shade more interested than usual. They seemed, this time, to be looking at him as if he were a person, not merely a Junior E. When he turned away from them to greet the three Juniors, who, along with himself, ranked the club-room privileges, he became certain of his impressions. Their faces were frankly envious.

Eden was to be his problem!

He'd hoped for it. Even half expected it. Yet all the way through his shower, dressing, coming down the elevator from his apartment, he'd been nagged with the fear he might not be considered; that the grief of Linda and her rise above it would lead only to anticlimax. By the time he'd got to the club-room door, followed by his orderly, he had already conditioned himself to disappointment.

Now he subdued his elation while he told his orderly what he wanted for breakfast.

"You fellows join me in something?" he asked both juniors and seniors.

"A second cup of coffee," Wong agreed.

"A second bourbon," old McGinnis said drily.

The juniors shook their heads negatively. Yesterday they had been his constant companions, only a few degrees below him in accomplishment, pushing rapidly to become his equal competitors for the next solo. Today, this morning, there was already a gap between them and him, a chasm they would make no move to bridge until they had earned the right. They seated themselves at another table, apart.

"Of course we haven't asked you if you want this Eden problem," McGinnis commented while orderlies placed food and drink in front of them. "We ought to ask him, hadn't we, Wong?"

"First I should ask if either of you want it?" Cal said quickly. "Or perhaps Malinkoff, if he shows up."

"Malinkoff is too deep in something to come to the briefing," Wong said.

"Wong and I came only to help on your first solo, if we can," McGinnis said. "Always think a young fellow needs a little send-off. I remember, about fifty years ago, more or less. . . ."

"Worst thing to guard against," Wong interrupted, "is disappointment. This whole thing might add up to nothing. Might not turn out to be a genuine solo at all, just something any errand boy could do. In that case it wouldn't qualify you. You know that."

"Sure," Cal said. Naturally the problem would have to give real challenge. You didn't just go out and knock a home run to become an E. You tackled something outside the normal frame of reference, something that required original thinking, the E kind of thinking. You brought it off successfully. A given number of Seniors reviewed what you'd done. If they thought it was worth something, you got your big E. If they didn't, you tried again. And you didn't get it by default, just because somebody thought there should be a given quota of Seniors on the list.

"Little or big," he added, "I'd like the problem."

They said no more. He knew the score. He'd had twelve years of the most intensive training the E's themselves could devise. He knew that sometimes a Junior spent another ten or twelve years chasing down jobs which anybody on the spot could have solved if they'd used their heads a little before they ran on to something that challenged that training. He'd be lucky if this was big enough—but not too big.

That was in their minds, too.

5

On ordinary days there were only the usual few science reporters in the press room of E.H.Q. These held their jobs by the difficult compromise between the scientists' insistence upon accuracy and their publishers' equal insistence upon sensationalism.

Since the publisher paid the salary; since rewrite men, like television writers, maintained their own feeling of superiority to the mass by writing down to the level of a not very bright twelve-year-old; since the facts had to be trimmed and altered to fit the open space or time slot; even these reporters had a difficult time of maintaining the usual odds—that there is only a twenty-to-one chance that anything said in the newspapers or on the air may be accurate.

But on this morning the press room was crowded. In spite of all efforts of journalism to stir up old animosities to make news, or to force factional leaders into rashness which could not be settled without violence; the various states of world government insisted upon negotiating ethnical differences amicably, and factional leaders persisted in keeping their heads. There had been no world-shaking discoveries made in the last week or so; the public no longer believed that changing a screw thread was exactly a scientific "break-through"; no real or imagined scandals seemed of such journalistic stature as to work the public into a frenzy of intolerance for one another's aberrations.

In such a dry spell, when advertisers were beginning to question circulation figures, and editors were racking their brains for a strong hate symbol to create interest, the delayed report from Eden came as a summer shower, that might be magnified into a flood.

EDEN SILENT quickly became COLONY FEARED LOST and progressed normally to COLONY WIPED OUT.

That there was no proof of loss or destruction bothered no one in journalism. If it did turn out this way, they'd have been on top of the news; and if it didn't, well, who remembers yesterday's headlines in the press of today's new hate and panic.

The public, with an established addiction to ever increasing daily doses of sensationalism, and deprived of its shots through this dry spell, snapped out of its apathy to greet this new thrill with vociferous calls to editors, wires to congressmen, telegrams to the Administration.

What are we doing about this colony that has been wiped out? Where is our space battle fleet? Who is going to be punished?

It was an overnight sensation, and on this morning following the news leak there could even be seen some secretaries to the writers for top commentators and columnists in the crowded press room.

Naturally these stood in little groups apart and associated only with each other to maintain the literary tradition of proper insulation from the realities of what was going on in the rest of the world. Obviously no first-rate writer could have afforded to appear in person not only because of damage to his stature lest it be noted he was doing his own spadework; but, more important, first-hand observation might limit his capacity for rationalizing the situation into the mold demanded by the bias of his commentator or columnist. It was always difficult to maintain author integrity when the facts did not support the sensationalism required by the employers, and best not to put oneself in such a position.

Now two of these secretaries could be seen over in a corner of the press room exchanging their views, probing one another for information. No one thought it curious they weren't trying to get the information from source for everyone in journalism understands the importance lies in what the competition is going to say, not in what happened.

"How long has it been since the first message came through, or didn't?"

"Fourteen hours, about."

"We could have had a rescue fleet out there by now."

"To rescue 'em from what?"

"Whatever's wrong."

"I understand an assistant attorney general is checking into it."

"So Gunderson's still gunning for the E's, eh?"

"Has he ever let up since he became attorney general? Gripes his soul he can't arrest them for not doing what he wants, or for doing what he doesn't want."

"How'd they ever get immune, anyhow?"

"Skip class that day in history?"

"Must've."

"Vague, myself. Right after the insurrection. Seems there were two powers, Russia and America. The people of the world got fed up, gave a pox to both their houses, boiled over, formed a world government. Somehow the scientists got in their licks in the turmoil, pointed out that scientists who have to confine their discoveries to what suits the ideology of the non-scientists can only find limited solutions."

"Quite a deal."

"Could only happen in a world turmoil, when everything was fluid. Anyhow, they got away with it, for a certain group, Extrapolators, had to be free to extrapolate without fear of reprisal."

"Boy, something. Imagine. Take any dame you want. Nobody can squawk. Take any money, riches you want. Nobody can stop it."

"Funny thing. Nothing like that happens. Idea seems to be that when you don't have to fight against restrictions, they aren't important any more. At least not to an E."

"Guess that's why one of 'em pointed out that police are the major cause of crime."

"Whether he was right or wrong, that's what sent Gunderson into a tail spin. I wouldn't be surprised but what he's a little hipped on that subject. He'll get 'em one of these days. Even an E can made a mistake, and when one of 'em does, he'll be there."

"I dunno, the public has a lot of hero-worship for the E. Pretty tough for any politician to buck that."

"The public! You know as well as I do—they think what we tell 'em to think, you and me."

"You think that's why he's got a man out here on this Eden thing? Looking for a mistake?"

"Maybe. Maybe not. He just never passes up the chance that maybe this time he can grab something."

"Between Gunderson and the E's, I'll take the E's."

"Your boss feel the same way?"

"Far as I know."

"But if your boss changed his mind, you would have an agonizing reappraisal."

"Well, sure. A guy's got to eat."

6

The west wall of the E club room began to glow, lose its appearance of solidity. Cal signaled his orderly to lift away his table. Now, where the west wall had been, another room seemed to join this one, an office. A large man in a brown suit made an entrance through the door of the office and sat down back of the desk. His face was drawn with weariness.

"I am Bill Hayes," he said. "Sector administration chief of the Eden area. I am acting moderator of this review. We follow the usual rules of procedure. I just want to say, as an aside, that the scientists involved in this problem have been up all night reviewing every known fact about Eden. We ask the indulgence of the E's not only for the kind of knowledge that may prove too little, but for any strain caused by trying to assemble such massive data into order in so short a time.

"For the press, let me say we are aware of some questions of why we didn't immediately send out a fleet of ships as soon as the call failed to come through. A military man does not rush troops into battle until he has some idea of what he must oppose; even a plumber needs to get some idea of the problem before he knows what tools to take with him. It would serve no constructive purpose to rush an unprepared fleet out to rescue, and might prove the highest folly."

All over E.H.Q., in the various buildings where anybody was directly concerned, the same effect would be taking place as appeared here in the club room. The tri-di screen wall would seem to join the room of the person speaking. A pressed button signaled the desire to speak, and like the chairman of a meeting, Bill Hayes decided whom to recognize. It was a way to conduct a meeting of two or three thousand people as intimately as a small conference.

"The E's have signaled they are ready for the Eden briefing," Hayes continued formally. He faded out his own office, and was immediately replaced by an astrophysics laboratory. The review of Eden was under way.

With sky charts, pointers, math formulae and many references to documentation, the astrophysicist established the celestial position of Ceti relative to Earth, and its second planet Ceti II —popularly called, he had heard, Eden. For his part, bitterly, he preferred a little less popularizing of scientific data, a little more exactitude. He would, therefore, continue to call it Ceti II.

He reminded Cal of certain teachers in schools he had been asked to leave back in his ugly duckling days. How didactically, positively, they clung to their exactitudes—like frightened little children in a chaotic world too big for them to face, hanging on to mother's skirts, something safe, sure, dependable.

The astrophysicist continued, at considerable length, to establish the position of Ceti II to his own complete satisfaction.

In his own mind Cal willingly conceded that, at least in terms of third-dimensional space-time continuum, Eden could be found where the man said it was. Then he reminded himself, sternly, that the essence might be that Eden was there no longer; that he'd better pay closest attention to everything said, however positive and didactic, lest he find his own mind closed to a solution. He reminded himself that, after all, these people had worked all night for his benefit, while he lay peacefully in Linda's arms.

He reminded himself that one little bit of datum, one little phrase, carelessly heard now, might mean his success or failure.

Didactic pedantry has its place in science, and these were scientists, not vaudeville performers. Silently, he apologized to the lot of them.

A geophysicist took over the review. He quickly got down out of space to the surface of Eden. Personally he didn't mind calling it Eden, just so all the purists knew he was referring to Ceti II. This was supposed to be humorous, and he waited until all the viewers had had a chance to chuckle with him.

If the astrophysicist signaled his demand for a retraction and apology for this public ridicule, Bill Hayes apparently didn't feel it worth breaking up the review to oblige him.

After he had enjoyed his own humor, the geophysicist did present his capsule of knowledge with excellent brevity.

There were no large continents. Instead, there were thousands of islands, so many that the land mass roughly equaled the sea surface. The islands had not been counted, he admitted, and then needlessly explained that Eden had been discovered only ten years ago. Since universe exploration was expanding much faster than properly qualified scientists could follow to catalogue conditions, details such as this had been left for future colonists to complete.

He took time out to complain that the younger generation was too dazzled by glamor and wanted to become entertainment stars, sports stars, jet jockeys exploring space, and there weren't enough going into the solid sciences to keep up with the work to be done.

A biophysicist interposed here and stated that his research with the injection of uric acid into rats caused a marked rise in intelligence, and if the Administration would just pay attention and let him have the grant he was asking, he felt confident that research in how to change the human kidney structure would take us a long mutant leap ahead toward humans with super-intelligence.

Bill Hayes cut him off as tactfully as possible and suggested that the Eden problem was here and now, and perhaps we should get that one out of the way first. Both scientists, by their expressions, indicated that they did not appreciate being frustrated, hampered, driven—but they did comply.

Back to Eden they went.

The climate was something like that of the Hawaiian area. Partly this was due to the variable plane rotation that heated all parts evenly, partly due to favorable flow of ocean currents. It had been noted that there was such an interweaving of cool and warm currents all over the globe that a relatively even temperature was maintained throughout. Some differential in spots, of course, enough to cause rainfall, but no real violence of storms, not as we classified hurricanes, typhoons, tornadoes here on Earth.

"Probably no sudden storm to wipe out the colony before they could send news, then," Wong suggested in an aside to Cal.

"Or a freak one did occur and they weren't prepared because it wasn't supposed to happen," Cal said.

Wong and McGinnis exchanged a quick glance, and Cal knew Wong had laid a little trap to see how easily he might be lulled into a premature conclusion.

The gravity was slightly less, the geophysicist was saying, but only to the extent that man, newly arrived from Earth, walked with a springier step, didn't tire as quickly. Not enough to cause nausea, even to the inexperienced. The oxygen content of the air, in fact the whole make-up of the air, was so close to Earth quality there were no breathing adaptations necessary.

So much for generalities. He went on to document them with exactitudes. He teamed up with a meteorologist to explain the distribution of rainfall in spite of lack of frigid and torrid air masses. Cal's doubt was not appeased. Weather prediction was about on a par with race-horse handicapping, and easy to explain after it happened.

Eventually the geophysicist and the meteorologist completed their duet to the accompaniment of oceanographers and geologists.

A chorus of botanists replaced them on the tri-di screen, the major theme of their epic being that an astonishing proportion of the plant forms bore edible fruit, nuts, seeds, leaves, stems, roots, flowers. A choir of zoologists joined their voices here to point out the large number of small meat animals, fish, and crustaceans—with the whole thing sounding like a pean of thanksgiving.

After two hours, the condensed information added up to a most interesting fact. In essence, due to quite *natural* conditions—odd how much the scientists seemed to need stressing the word "natural"—Eden was more favorable to easy human life than Earth!

Cal leaned forward. Here was the spot where some student or apprentice might distinguish himself by asking an embarrassing question or so. Say the range of easily possible conditions on any given planet was a scale ten miles in length. Then that area on the scale where man could exist without artificial aids would still be less than a hair's breadth. And now to find a planet more nearly perfect for man than the one on which he evolved. . . .

Or were the students considering this too obvious to mention? He decided to nudge them a little. Sometimes a discussion of the too obvious brought out things not obvious at all.

"How frequently," he asked, when Hayes had cut him in, "do we find a mass revolving in such a manner that its poles revolve at right angles to its forward revolution, so there is no real pole?"

"It requires near-perfect roundness, and an even distribution of land and water masses, such as we have on Ceti II," the first astrophysicist answered.

"How frequently do we find that?" Cal repeated.

"I know of no other," the astrophysicist replied shortly.

"Any evidence of tampering with those ocean currents to get them flowing so beneficially?" Cal asked.

"None yet discovered," an oceanographer cut in.

Well, at least he hadn't stated with positiveness that there hadn't been and couldn't be. But an anthropaleontologist inserted himself and spoiled the effect of open-mindedness.

"There is definitely no life form on Eden with sufficient intelligence for that," the man said, "nor has there ever been. Such a feat would require enormous engineering works. Such works under the ocean would be matched by comparable works on land, and would therefore show up in our aerial surveys, however ancient and overgrown."

Cal sighed softly to himself. The human kind of civilization, yes, that would have left traces. But what of some other kind? Perhaps a deep sea kind that had never come out upon the land? Never mind the arguments that such a civilization could not have developed—that was looking at it from the human point of view again. Had man grown so accustomed to not finding comparable intelligence anywhere in the universe he had begun to discount, or forget, there could be?

The review went on and on. The zoologist sketched in the prevalent animals and fish forms, showed there was nothing in land animals higher than a large rodent, no sea mammals at all, no fish larger than the tarpon. Nothing at all to hint at a line of primates.

A bacteriologist exclaimed at length over the similarity of minute life forms to those on Earth, and used the occasion to again expound the old theory of space-floating life spores to seed all favorable matter, and thus develop similar forms through evolution, wherever found. Quickly and tactfully Bill Hayes nudged him back on the track before the expected storm of controversy could break out.

Then there was a short lunch time, but not a leisurely one. Quite aside from the emergency of what might be happening to the colonists, there was growing clamor from the people and pressure from various governmental bodies to get off the dime and get going—rescue those people, or, cynically, at least make a show of action to quell the flood of telegrams. E.H.Q. resisted the pressures in favor of doing a workmanlike job in preparation for a genuine rescue instead of a haphazard show, but was mindful of them nevertheless.

7

Anyone who has witnessed even so much as a traffic-court trial cannot help but realize that "government by law instead of man" is a mere political phrase without meaning in reality. The ascendancy of me-and-mine over you-and-yours runs so deep in the human psyche that abstract idealisms must always take second place where such ascendancy is threatened. Thus we see that the belly-crawler, meek and subservient to the judge, comes off with a token sentence while the man who attempts to maintain his pride, his rights, his self-respect gets the book thrown at him.

No practical attorney is unaware that the judgment of his case depends largely upon who presides, the whims, the prejudices, the moods, the viewpoint of the judge; and that the law merely provides justification for the imposition of those whims, moods, prejudices, and viewpoints.

And ambitions.

The announcement at E.H.Q. that a Junior E would be given this problem gave Gunderson's man the opening he had hoped to find. A hurried call to the capitol and a brief conversation with Gunderson himself confirmed his conclusions. Perhaps the E was above all law, and it might not be expedient to challenge that right now, but immunity did not necessarily extend to the Junior E.

In view of the known ambitions of certain judges, it should not be difficult to make a test case of this—whether the E's had a right to jeopardize a colony of human beings by assigning an unqualified man to the problem.

A question, too, of who had jurisdiction over the Juniors, the apprentices, the students. How far down the line did the mantle of the E extend to protect those not yet qualified? How far out did the Administration of E.H.Q. extend to substitute for government? How much of a state within a state had E.H.Q. become?

Now, while the public was clamoring for action, and E.H.Q. was, instead, droning on through a mass of inconsequential detail, now while public sentiment was crystallizing, or could be crystallized into placing human welfare over science procedures, now was the time.

It was not difficult to find a judge who was predisposed to favor the request of the attorney general.

8

After lunch at E.H.Q., the colonizing administrator took over the review.

The precolonizing scientists had not been trapped by the obviously favorable aspects of Eden into neglecting their full duties. No indeed! they had given the full routine of tests and had come up with exactly nothing that might be unfavorable to man, at least not more so than on Earth.

Colonization had followed the usual plan. Fifty professional colonists had been sent out to Eden. They knew their jobs. They were temperamentally suited to the work.

As usual, they were to live there for five years, leaning as lightly as possible on Earth supplement. Their prime purpose was to adapt primitive ecology to human needs, how it could be done. It was not the job of this first colony to explore, to catalogue. They were expected to do only what any pioneer does—endure, exist, and prove it possible.

In honesty the colonizing administrator had to point out there had been more than the usual dissatisfaction from this colony. The burden of their complaint was that they found living too easy. They were professionals, accustomed to challenge.

They had first recommended, then demanded, that they be transferred and the planet given over to the second-phase colonists.

They complained they were dying on the vine, that easy living was making farmers and storekeepers out of them, that they were getting soft, ruined by disuse of their talents for meeting and coping with hostile conditions. There had even been threats that one of these days they would all pile into their ship and come back home. So far he had stopped them by threats of his own, that he would personally see they never got another assignment.

He had resisted their demands. Five years was a short enough time. Some organisms took longer than that to develop in the human body or mind, to make their inimical presence known. Some did not show up until the second or third generation; which was the reason for the second-phase colonists, to live there for three generations, before the planet could be opened to young John Smith and his wife Mary who dreamed of owning a little chicken ranch out away from it all. He had argued that boredom might be just the very inimical condition they were having to test.

Cal felt a twinge of disappointment here. Perhaps the dissatisfied colonists had merely gone on strike! Unable to get satisfaction from their administrator, they chose not to communicate as a means of drawing attention, getting an investigation of their plight. Drastic, perhaps, but man had been known to do drastic things before when he felt treated unfairly.

This seemed such a likely solution that for a moment he let his disappointment override his interest. Such would be an administrative hassle, nothing to challenge an E at all, not even a junior.

Still, it might not be the solution. He had better listen to the whole of the problem.

The colonists had chosen a large island for their first settlement. In the center was a small mountain. It had been given the name of Crystal Palace Mountain because it was crested with an outcropping of amethystine quartz-crystal structures in *natural* pillars, domes, arches, spires.

Like spokes of a wheel radiating out from the hub, ridges fell

51

away from this mountain, and in between the ridges there lay fertile valleys watered by perpetual streams.

It was in one of these valleys, about halfway between the mountain and the sea, that the colonists settled. Some bucolic wit had named the first settlement Appletree, because there they would gain knowledge, and everybody knows that the apple was the Garden of Eden's fruit of knowledge. No one quite knew when the name Eden was first applied to the planet. Suddenly, during the first scientific expedition, everyone was referring to it that way.

"For exactitude," the administrator said diplomatically. "Of course we still designate it as Ceti II."

As was customary, the colony had communicated multitudes of progress pictures over the space-jump band. Here was the valley before they had started to fell trees. Here it was in progress of clearing. Here they were converting the trees into lumber for houses. Here were the first houses so that some could move out of the living quarters in the ship. Here they were uprooting the stumps, turning the sod, planting Earth seed. These were barns for the cattle and horses sent with them from Earth.

A collection of community buildings came next in the series of photographs, and finally there was the whole village of Appletree, with a collection of small farms surrounding it. The pictures showed it all as ideal for man as a distant view of a rural valley in Ohio. Productive, progressive, and peaceful—from a distance.

But back of the post-card scene, human psychology progressed normally also.

The reporting psychologist was most emphatic on this issue. His department would have been most alarmed had differences and schisms *not* developed. *That* would have been an abnormality calling for investigation.

Differences in outlook became apparent in spite of the common temperament and experience of the group. Little personal enmities developed and grew. Sympathizers drew together in little groups, each group considering its stand to be the right one, and therefore all who disagreed wrong.

The psychologist said he was sure all viewing would remember the classical picture of primitive Earth man at first awareness. He stands upon a hill and looks about him. There comes the astonishing realization that he can see about the same distance in all directions.

"Why," he exclaims to himself, "I must be at the very center of creation!"

His awe and wonder was to grow. Wherever he went, he found he was still at the center of things. There could be only one conclusion.

"Because I am always at the center of things, I must be the most important event in all creation!"

Still later comes another realization.

"Those who are with me, and are therefore a part of me-and-mine, are also at the center of things and share my importance. Those who are not with me, and not a part of me-and-mine, are not at the center of things, and are therefore of an inferior nature!"

It could readily be seen—the psychologist was allowing a note of dryness to enter his comments—that the bulk of man's philosophy, religion, politics, social values, and yes, too often even his scientific conclusions, was based upon this egocentric notion; the supreme importance and rightness of me-and-mine ascendant at the center of things, opposed to those who are not a part of me-and-mine, on the outside, and therefore inferior.

There must have been a signal from Bill Hayes, for the psychologist left the generalities behind and came back to the issue.

The very ease of living on Eden fostered the growth of schisms, for there was no common enemy to band the group into one solid me-and-mine organism—the audience would recall that when Earth was divided into nations it had always been imperative to find a common enemy in some other nation; that this was the only cohesive force man had been able to find to keep the nation from disintegrating.

Another nudge.

Factions took shape on Eden and clashed in town meetings. At last, as expected, some dissident individuals and family groups could no longer tolerate the irritation of living in the same neighborhood with the rest. These broke off from the main colony, and migrated across the near ridge to settle in an adjacent valley.

Psychologically, it was a most satisfactory development, playing out in classical microcosm the massive behavior of total man. For, as everyone knew, had men ever been able to settle their differences, had man been able to get along peacefully with himself, he might have developed no civilization at all.

Man's inability to stand the stench of his own kind was the most potent of all forces in driving him out to the stars.

Bill Hayes, a weary and red-eyed moderator now, apparently decided he could no longer stand the stench of the psychologist and abruptly cut him off. He himself took over the summation. It boiled down to a simple statement.

The colonists had reported everything that happened, of significance or not. These reports had all been thoroughly sifted in the normal course of E.H.Q.'s daily work as they were received. They had been collated and extended both by human and machine minds to detect any subtle trends away from norm.

There had been nothing, absolutely nothing. The reports might as well have originated somewhere near Eugene, Oregon. They were about as unusual as a Saturday night bath back on the farm.

Then silence. Sudden, inexplicable silence.

9

"It bothers me, it bothers me a lot," Cal said to the two E's, following the review, "that Eden should be more favorable to effortless human existence than Earth."

He snapped on the communicator and asked the ship be in readiness for take-off.

McGinnis and Wong looked at one another.

"You think it might have been the original Garden of Eden?" Wong asked. His face was impassive. "It fits, you know. Man was banished from an ideal condition and forced to live by the sweat of his brow."

"Not that so much," Cal said. "Not unless the whole concept of evolution is haywire, and we're reasonably sure it isn't that far off. Probably the colonists have gone on strike, but I still keep thinking that when we want to catch rats we set a trap with a better food than they can get normally."

There was a twinkle in McGinnis's eye.

"You think Eden is an alluring trap, especially baited to catch human beings?" he asked.

"I don't exactly think that. I just keep wondering," Cal answered.

They were interrupted by a diffident yet insistent knock on the door. This in itself was such a violation of E.H.Q. rules, never to interrupt the thinking of an E, that all three stopped talking. The three Juniors, who had been sitting by, listening, arose from their seats and stood facing the door. The orderlies looked to the E's for instruction. At a nod from McGinnis, one of them walked over to the door and opened it.

Bill Hayes was standing there, flushed with embarrassment.

"Your pardon, E's," he said hurriedly. "I'm just an errand boy, under instruction from General Administration. We have been served with a court injunction to prevent assignment of a Junior to the Eden matter."

Cal froze in alarm and disappointment. At the last moment to have his chance snatched away from him. He should have gone immediately the review was over, without waiting for any advice McGinnis and Wong might care to give. Now. . . .

McGinnis caught his eye and gave a slight nod toward a door that opened on another hallway. He flashed a command with his eyes to get going, then turned back to Hayes.

"I was unaware that the E's must heed court orders," he said frostily.

"It's a question of where civil jurisdiction stops and E jurisdiction takes over," Hayes explained nervously. "While the colonists are employed by E.H.Q., and under their direction, it is held they are also Earth citizens, with citizen rights. Civil authority feels it must answer for their welfare."

"I thought restrictions upon the E were removed by act of World Congress some seventy years ago," Wong said mildly.

"The injunction makes it clear there is no restriction upon the Senior E; just the Junior, who really isn't an E yet."

"It is the decision of the E's that a Junior will handle this problem," McGinnis said, and turned his back as if that settled the matter.

Hayes cleared his throat nervously.

"I'm sorry," he said. "If it were up to me. . . . Well, the argument before the court ran this way: That where there is no restriction upon the E in arriving at a solution, there is also no compulsion upon civil authority to adopt that solution. They cited instances . . . Well, any number of instances. It seems. . . ."

Cal heard no more. He had been pacing the room, and now, while Hayes's perspiring attention was focused imploringly on Wong and McGinnis, he slipped out the door.

The orderly at that door raised a finger in salute, and at Cal's request quickly wheeled a hall-car from a storage closet.

"Take me out to the Eden ship," Cal said quietly. "You know where it is?"

"Yes," the orderly answered. He took his place at the controls and Cal slipped into the seat beside him.

They sped through the halls at maximum speed, out the rear exit of the E building, down the maze of ramps and out across the landing field to the entrance of the ship.

Cal expected to see guards posted there to enforce the injunction, but none were in evidence. As they drew up to the open door, he saw Lynwood and Norton, pilot and engineer, standing just inside waiting for him. There was no strain in their faces to show they had received orders not to take off with him.

He climbed out of the car, and with another nod the orderly drove it back to the E building. Henceforward the ship's crew would be the E's orderlies.

Cal climbed the short ramp and entered the ship.

"You have clearance to take off at once?" he asked Lynwood.

Lynwood nodded. "Since early morning," he answered.

"Fine. Let's get going," Cal said. "I'm in a hurry, of course," he added with a grin.

"Of course," the two men answered, then seeing his grin, relaxed and returned it. Apparently this E was human.

It took only a minute for them to reach the control room, where Louie sat in his navigator's cubby; and only ten more seconds for the ship to lift clear. And still no command came over the radio to halt them.

Someone in civil authority had slipped. Had Gunderson really felt that a simple injunction would stop everything, that the E's would not challenge this encroachment? Was he playing some deeper game, allowing the Junior to slip through his fingers in the hope he would louse up the Eden rescue, add strength to the campaign to bring the E's back under civil control—his control?

Or had someone genuinely slipped?

The command to halt, turn around, and return to base did not come until their second hop had brought them into the Mars orbit. Then it came from space police in charge of shipping traffic at that point.

"I am under orders from E.H.Q. to proceed," Tom answered, after a quick, questioning look at Cal.

"The attorney general's office orders you to halt," the voice commanded.

Tom looked at Cal again, questioning. This was bucking the federal government, his license wouldn't be worth the paper it was written on if he ignored the order. To say nothing of any other punishment they might choose to hand him.

"Keep going," Cal answered shortly. "And make your next jump as quickly as you can."

"I am under orders to keep going," Tom answered the police. If he refused the request of an E, a lifetime of work would go down the drain.

Over in his seat, Frank Norton's fingers were speeding through the intricate pattern of setting up the next jump. He and Louie were working as one man.

"I am under orders to disable you if you refuse," the police warned.

"We have an E on board," Tom answered. "You'd be risking a lot."

"I am advised he is a Junior E," the voice said in clipped speech. "Not such a risk."

"Far as I'm concerned," Tom answered laconically, "he's an E. I have to follow his orders."

He nodded to Frank who touched the jump switch. There was

an instant silence. They were at the approach to the asteroid belt.

"They can get us here," Louie spoke up. "We have to give over controls so they can take us through. No chart can keep up to the microsecond on these asteroid movements. They have to calculate a path in short hops, and take us through a step at a time. I keep saying there ought to be an expressway out of the solar system, but. . . ."

"What about a good long jump at right angles?" Cal asked. "Get over it instead of through it?"

"It's illegal," Louie complained.

"Our necks are aready out," Tom said quietly.

"Okay, you're the boss. But I'll have to figure it. It takes time to figure it."

"Well, get going on it."

"There's stuff all over," Louie explained. "Not just a band, like most people think. The asteroids have moved at right angles, too. Not so thick, but there's a globe of stuff, not just a belt. Maybe a bunch of little jumps."

"We can't start making them until you figure them, Louie," Frank reminded him.

The radio gave its hum of life, and a voice came through.

"We have orders from space police not to escort you through, to turn you back."

"This is an E ship, with an E on board. His command is to come through," Tom said.

"I just work here," the voice answered as if it were bored and tired. "I take my orders from Space Control."

Tom looked over at Louie. Louie apparently caught the look out of a corner of his eye, and impatiently waved a finger not to bother him. His other hand was speeding through the movements of manipulating the astrocalculator. Then he nodded his head, still not looking up, and the co-ordinates flashed in front of Frank. Now, as rapidly as Louie, Frank set up the pattern of the jump band.

"I take my orders from the E's," Tom answered in a voice that matched the boredom, tiredness. Then with a nod from Frank, "Now!" he said.

There was silence again.

"It's going to add at least an hour," Louie complained. "I've got to pick my way through this muck."

"We've got time now," Tom answered easily. "Not likely they can find us out here, away from the regular lanes."

"Not unless we run across a prowl ship," Louie said. "You know there's some smuggling, and now and then a shipping company thinks it can beat the rap, not pay the toll, by doing the same thing we're doing. The prowl patrol is on to all the tricks. We're not the first ones to try it."

"Just keep figuring, Louie," Tom said.

"All right, all right!" Louie quarrelled back.

Tom looked at Cal and grimaced.

"Louie's all right," he said. "Just has to complain."

"I'm sure of it," Cal answered with a grin.

It took closer to two hours. They had no way of knowing how many times the space police had made a fix on their position only too late to catch them hovering there. There must have been some fix made and a pretty careful calculation of where they could go next, for as they neared the outer moons of Jupiter the radio crackled into life again.

"This is your last warning. We intend to board you and take over. We will disintegrate your ship if you resist."

Cal took the microphone in his own hand to answer.

"We intend to keep going," he said. "This is a jurisdictional dispute between the attorney general's office and E.H.Q. We will not allow you to board us, and I suggest you get confirmation of orders to disintegrate us directly from the attorney general in person. Meanwhile you can pass the buck to your Saturn patrol if those orders are confirmed."

Tom nodded to Frank, and the next jump key was pressed.

In the Saturn field, still another voice came through. "Orders from the attorney general himself are to allow you to proceed. Say, Lynwood, what is this all about?"

"Some sort of petty squabble over who gives orders to who," Lynwood answered. "I just work here," he added tiredly.

"Well," said the voice. "So do I. Guess they'll fight it out in the courts now. You understand, we had our orders."

"You understand, so did I." Tom answered.

"Sure," the voice answered, and cut out.

Cal wondered whether the orders to disintegrate had been a bluff. Would the attorney general have dared disintegrate a ship with even a Junior E on board? Maybe it had been just a threat of the local police, one they didn't expect to have called.

Or maybe he had played directly into the attorney general's hands by defying him, and getting that defiance on record was what the man had wanted.

Whatever it was, the Eden matter had become bigger than merely finding out what had happened to some colonists. Whatever it was, he'd better find a successful solution, because the attorney general was counting on him to fail. And if he did fail, certainly the position of the Junior E would be altered, and possibly a deep thrust into the very heart of the Senior E position, as well.

10

Louie was right. After they cleared the solar system there was no trouble getting *to* Eden. And there was no trouble circumnavigating the globe while still in space.

Closer, but still outside the atmosphere in their surveying spiral, they had no trouble in locating the island with Crystal Palace Mountain at its center. There was only one such spot on Eden, and in their telescope viewer its crystalline spires and minarets sparkled back at them like a diamond set in jade.

The trouble began when they hovered over the location, when they amplified their magnification to get a close look at the Appletree village before dropping down to land.

Louie found the right valley. He said it was the right valley, and he stuck to his claim stubbornly.

But there was no settlement there. No sign there had ever been.

Louie could see that for himself, they told him. There was nothing but virgin land. The trees were undisturbed, and old. There were splashes of rolling meadows spotted here and there by other trees, untilled meadows sloping downward from the ridges to the river. And not a blemish nor scar to show that man had ever landed there.

"Fine thing," Norton chaffed him. "Fine navigation, Louie. Get us clear across the universe in great shape, and then you can't even find the landing field."

But Louie was in no mood for banter. He wished Tom would go back and hold the manual controls of the ship instead of letting it hover on automatic. He wished Cal would go back to his stateroom and think. He wished Frank Norton would shut up. He wished they wouldn't all stand over him, reading his charts over his shoulder.

In irritated silence he reduced the viewscope dimensions to scale, and snapped a picture of the whole island. He took the fresh picture, still moist from its self-developing camera, and laid it beside the chart. Wordlessly, for the benefit of them all, he traced his pencil over the outlines of the chart and their duplicates in the picture. As in comparing fingerprints, he flicked his pencil at the points of identity. There were far too many to ignore. He poked the point of his pencil at Appletree where it was located on the chart. Then he picked out the same location in the picture.

It was not the science of navigation that was wrong.

"It's just one of those dirty tricks life plays on a fellow," Tom said over Cal's shoulder. "You got us in the right place, Louie, but probably in the wrong time slot. You've warped us right out of our own time, and Eden hasn't been discovered yet. Maybe won't be for another million years. Maybe, back on Earth, man is just discovering fire."

"Yeah," Norton agreed. "Or maybe in the wrong dimension. You and your fancy navigation. Now you take a midgit-idgit navigating machine. It wouldn't know how to pull such fancy short cuts. Take a little longer, maybe, but when we got there we'd be there."

They were both talking nonsense and knew it. Time and dimensional travel were still purely theoretical. Louie ignored the ribbing with elaborate patience.

"You know what I think," he asked seriously. "I think the whole thing's a hoax. I'll betcha there never was any settlement there. I'll betcha the colonists have pulled a whingding all the way through."

63

"There's a whole raft of pictures to show they were there," Frank reminded him.

"Pictures!" Louie answered scornfully. "You think they couldn't fake pictures?" He thought for a moment. "And where's their ship, their escape ship?" he asked as a clincher. "They didn't like it here and have gone off somewhere else, and then covered up by sending reports and pictures on how things would have developed if they'd stayed."

There was a sense of unreality in the whole conversation. Cal let the talk flow on, knowing it was a reaction to shock. What if a modern ocean liner pulled into the harbor of New York—to find an untouched Manhattan Island in its virgin state?

It couldn't happen, therefore it wasn't to be treated seriously.

"Better set up communication with Earth," Cal said quietly.

In E science the unpredictable, the incredible, the illogical could happen at any time. With a mind more open to acceptance of this, he had felt the run of shock sooner. For them, the shock impact was delayed since their minds rejected the illogical as unreal. For him the human shock came at once, and then, as E thinking took over, passed off.

"Sure, Cal," Lynwood agreed. It was a measure of their acceptance that they had quite normally fallen into using his first name.

On the emergency signal it took less than three minutes to clear through eleven light-years to E.H.Q.—and then sixteen minutes for the operator at base to find Bill Hayes.

"Sector Chief Hayes here," the voice said at last through the speaker.

"Gray here, on the Eden matter," Cal answered. "Any other E's available?"

"Hm-m," Hayes answered. "Wong has picked up on a problem in the Pleiades sector, and left this morning. Malinkoff has given out word not to disturb him if the whole universe falls apart. That leaves McGinnis, who, I believe, is spending his time working on the defense against the injunction by Gunderson. An example of the way petty restrictions can bring a fine mind down to trivial problems. But he said call him if you need him."

"Please," Cal said. "And you might stay on while I talk to him, if you're not busy."

"Sure, E Gray, sure," Hayes answered. "I'm flashing the operator to locate McGinnis. Seen anything of the police ship, yet? I understand one is following to observe what you do."

"I'm sure it will be a big help," Cal said drily. "Not that it matters, so long as it doesn't get in the way."

McGinnis came on at that point.

"I'm not yelling for help, yet," Cal told him. "But here's what it is like at this end." He sketched in the details, and heard a sharp gasp at the other end from Hayes.

"Now I'd like to stay on this problem," he concluded his brief summary. "But somewhere there's fifty colonists in trouble because this whole thing is out of focus. I'm not a full E, and maybe their lives are more important than my ambition to do a solo job. Certainly more important. Then, trivial as it is, we'd be playing right into Gunderson's hands if we've sent out a boy to do a man's job."

"Dismiss the Gunderson side of it," McGinnis said drily. "It's inconsequential to the main issue. As for that, I don't know any more than you do. There's never been anything like this. Colonists have been wiped out on other planets, sure; but what happened left traces. This one is an oddball, and I'd say you're as well equipped to handle it as anybody else."

"I don't—I don't understand this at all," Hayes said in a worried voice.

"Who does?" Cal asked. "I'd say set up for continuous communication. I'll leave it wide open here, so that everything we say will come through. Then, if anything should happen to us, you'll have the record up to that point."

"It's the only thing we can do," Hayes agreed.

"If you think I should come out there to stand by, I'll do it," McGinnis said. But the tone of his voice said he hoped Cal would shoulder the full responsibility, not weaken out of a chance at a real solo.

"I'm not crying uncle, yet," Cal said. "But I may have to take you up on the offer. I hope not."

"But do you *know* anything is wrong?" Hayes asked incredulously. He was having the same trouble facing the reality as the ship's crew.

"If you were flying to Los Angeles and found only desert where the city is supposed to be, you might assume something was wrong," Cal answered drily. "But I don't know what it is. Do you have a recorder set up, so I can begin trying to find out?"

"Yes, yes E Gray," Hayes said hurriedly. He was suddenly conscious that he had been interrupting an E conversation, not once but several times. "Pardon the intrusions. It was just that. . . ."

"I understand," Cal reassured him.

When Cal stood up from the communicator, the eyes of the crew were on him. Overhearing his conversation with Earth had sobered them, made reality come closer.

"You think it might be a mirage?" Tom asked. "Some freak air current reflecting from another island and superimposing over this one?" Then he answered himself. "No. I guess it isn't. There aren't enough discrepancies."

"Let's pan down to the ground with the scanner," Cal said. "Take it slow over the area where the village is supposed to be."

Glad to be doing something with his hands, Lynwood twisted the controls to take them instantly, in magnification, to a distance slightly above the tops of the trees. The automatic pilot caused the ship to drift with the rotation of the planet, keeping them in fixed relative position.

They scanned the ground rod by rod. There were expanses of heavy tree and bush growth that they could not penetrate. Some of these trees grew where the pictures showed cleared fields, buildings, truck gardens, cattle pastures.

"Those big trees didn't grow up in a month, since the last

colonist report," Louie said positively. He still clung to his belief that it was all a hoax.

Cal made no comment. He was intent on the scanner screen. There were heavy foliage spots, but there were also bare areas covered by a soft, springy turf and patches of wild flowers. But there was no sign of man or his works. There was not so much as a board, the glint of a nail, not a furrow, not even the scar of a campfire. And no indication that there had ever been.

In the sandy patches along the banks of the small meandering river, there was not even a footprint.

They swept the scanner down the valley.

"Wait a minute," Cal said. "There are some cows and horses." He held the scanner fixed while they studied the animals. In two small herds, the animals grazed contentedly near a patch of woods.

"We're in the right time slot, then," Tom said, with an attempt to pick up the spirit of treating it lightly. "They've been here. Else the cows and horses wouldn't be."

"Funny thing about those horses," Frank commented in a puzzled voice. "I grew up on a farm. Those are work horses, but field horses always have harness marks on them where the hair gets rubbed off or the skin gets calloused. If they used these horses for work, there ought to be collar and hames rubs on their necks. There ought to be worn streaks left by the traces on their sides. There isn't. Far as the evidence shows, they might have been wild all their lives."

"Whatever happened didn't seem to hurt them any," Cal agreed.

He swept the scanner on down the valley to the sandy shore of the sea. They were close enough to pick up the brown streaks of beached seaweed. A flock of shore birds were busy running up the sand away from the gentle, beaching waves, then following the water line back down to dig their beaks into the soft, wet sand for food. The birds showed no alarm, no sign of lurking presence near them.

Cal brought the scanner back up the valley and over to one of the ridges bordering it. High on the crest of the ridge, the undergrowth was less luxuriant than down in the valley.

And it was here they caught their first glimpse of a human being.

He was hunkered down behind some rocks at the crest, peering over them at the valley below. From the shape of his shoulders and back, the set of his head, they knew it to be a man. As far as they could tell, he had no clothes on. Apparently they had caught him at the moment of his arrival at the crest.

They watched him turn his head as he looked quickly, then searchingly, up and down the valley. They watched his hand come up to shade his eyes against the light from Ceti as he attempted to see into the dark patches of foliage where the village ought to be.

What he saw, or did not see, seemed to stun him. He squatted, as frozen as a statue for long moments. Then, on hands and knees, they saw him back away from the crest. Now they saw he did not wear even so much as a breechclout. When the height of the ridge concealed him from the other side, he sprang to his feet and began to run, zigzagging in the manner of an obstacle racer to avoid the bushes.

"Looks like they've decided to make a nudist colony of it," Lynwood commented.

"And faked the pictures so nasty-minded old Earth people wouldn't come out to break it up," Louie persisted.

"Then why should he be so scared," Frank asked.

"Notice that patch of bare dirt he's crossing?" Cal asked. "See the little spurts of dust when he puts his feet down? Now look behind him."

The three crewmen leaned closer to look over his shoulder at the scanning screen. Cal adjusted it minutely, to get a sharp focus on the ground.

"No footprints!" Lynwood exclaimed. "He doesn't leave any footprints!"

The three of them looked at Cal, wide-eyed. Cal didn't like what he saw in Louie's eyes. The habitual irritation and annoyance with life's little petty tricks was gone.

The look had been replaced with fear, and something more.

11

The naked man, running frantically down the side of the slope, disappeared momentarily under some taller growth, came out the other side of it still running. He leaped over a small ravine, stumbled, recovered himself, and disappeared again beneath a larger growth of trees. Below him, on his side of the ridge, there lay another valley with its own stream.

They caught one more fleeting glimpse, a mere flash of sunlight on tan skin. He was still heading downward in the direction of the stream. It was their last sight of him. They watched for a while longer, but he did not reappear under the green canopy of forest.

"Just a guess," Cal said. He spoke matter-of-factly in the hope the casualness would wash the fear and awe from Louie's eyes. "That's probably one of the dissident men who broke away from the main colony and set up housekeeping in this adjacent valley. Apparently the same things have happened to him as happened to the main colony, whatever it was.

"I'd guess it came as pretty much of a shock and he's just now worked up courage to scout the main valley. From that I'd say whatever happened wasn't very long ago, not more than a week. Just a guess."

None of the crew answered him. It was obviously not the case of a voyeur spying on others—not with the kind of excitement the running man had shown. Running away—that is.

"Let's drop down into the atmosphere," Cal suggested. "I'd assume it is breathable from the fact we've seen earth animals and a human being. Still we'd better make tests."

"Yeah," Louie said unexpectedly. "If the man isn't making any footprints maybe he isn't breathing, either." He tried to make it a joke, to fight his fear with self-derision. He didn't succeed. Nobody laughed. He swallowed hard and studied the charts again for no apparent reason.

Cal glanced quickly from Tom to Frank. A look at Norton's face showed him Frank wasn't very far behind Louie in the progress of shock. Perhaps, as with himself, it was Lynwood's sense of responsibility for his crew that was helping the pilot to maintain a better control. But there was a white line around Lynwood's mouth, running up the line of his jaw. Caused by clenching his teeth too tightly? Clenched, to keep them from chattering?

However experienced a man became, however dependable the reactions, one never knew how to predict reaction in the face of the completely unknown. Yet Cal knew that even if he asked any of the men if they feared to take him down it would be an insult never forgotten. It was their job to take an E where he wanted to go. It wouldn't be the first time they had gambled their lives on the judgment of an E.

"Oh-oh," Tom exclaimed. "We have company." He pointed to an indicator on the panel.

They swept the space around them with the scanner, and hovering off to one side they picked up another ship. They watched it for a while, as it hovered there. It made no move to come closer, no move to communicate with them.

"From its markings," Tom said at last, "I think that's a special investigation ship from the attorney general's office. Wonder what they're doing here?"

"To make first-hand observation of my failure," Cal said shortly. "Let's get on with our work."

Perhaps it helped the crew to realize they were not alone, that

71

whatever might happen to them would not only be heard on the E.H.Q. channel back to Earth, but would also be seen by these special observers. Perhaps it bucked them up a little to know that they were being watched, that faltering uncertainty would be noted and scorned. Perhaps it was the mechanical routine of air sampling and testing as they lowered the ship by degrees.

Norton grew more relaxed, more sure of himself. Lynwood handled the ship on manual control with ease, almost with flourish. But Louie's hands, gripping the edges of the chart table, still showed bloodless white at the knuckles. Perhaps because there was nothing for him to do at the moment, he alone wasn't snapping out of it.

The tests showed normal atmosphere. It checked exactly with the readings for this altitude established by the surveying scientists. To complete the record, Cal repeated them aloud each time so the open communicator would carry the information back to Earth where, by now, not only McGinnis and Hayes would be listening, but probably a group of scientists as well. Perhaps their hands, too, gripped the edges of tables, showed bloodless at the knuckles?

To wait, helplessly, eleven light-years away might create more tenseness than being right on the scene. Yet no voice came through the ship's speaker, either from Earth or from the observer's ship.

Perhaps McGinnis, forgetting his eighty years, wished now he were at Eden instead of Cal. Perhaps, mindful of his years, he didn't. He made no comment.

Tom dropped the ship lower and lower, each time pausing for an air sample. Each time they scanned the valley where the village of Appletree should be. There was no change. Now the unlikely idea of a superimposed mirage was dispelled. The disappearance of the colony was no trick of vision. The ship hovered, at the last, not more than fifty feet from the ground.

"Let's set her down, Tom," Cal said quietly.

Tom shrugged, as if that were the only thing left to do.

"You're the E," he said. His glance at Louie showed he was placing the responsibility not so much to avoid consequences for himself, nor so much to assure they were willing to follow an E's orders without question, as to remind Louie that there was, after all, an E with them. And if he were willing to face this unknown, they could hardly do less themselves.

But Louie's eyes were fixed in unblinking stare upon the ground below them. He was frozen and unheeding.

The actual landing was so flawless that Cal, involuntarily, glanced out of the port to confirm that they were no longer hovering.

"Might as well open up," he said. "Nothing has happened to us, so far."

Norton pushed a button. The exit hatch slipped open and the ramp unfolded and slid down to touch ground. Cal, flanked by Tom and Frank, looked through the opening into the woods beyond.

And while they looked, a man came from behind the screening protection of some shrubbery. He was followed by two other men. All of them were completely naked.

"You three stay inside the ship until I signal you to come out," Cal instructed. "If anything unusual happens to me, stand off from the planet until help can come from Earth. Don't be foolish and try to help me."

"You're the E," Tom repeated. When a man is outside his own knowledge, heroics might do more harm than good.

Cal stepped through the exit and walked slowly down the ramp.

The three colonists seemed in no panic. They walked toward him, also slowly, obviously in attempt at dignified control. Yet their faces were breaking into broad grins of relief and welcome.

Cal stepped off the ramp, took a step toward them, then it happened.

He heard breathless grunts of surprise and pain behind him. He whirled around. The three crewmen were lying awkwardly on the ground. There was no ship. The three crewmen where completely naked.

Cal felt the stirring of a breeze, and looked down quickly at his own body. He also was nude.

He turned back to face the colonists. They had stopped in front of him. Their joyous grins had been replaced by grimaces of despair.

Behind him the crewmen were in act of getting to their feet. A quick glance showed Cal none was hurt. Louie looked around, dazed and uncomprehending. There was not so much as a bent blade of grass to show where the ship's weight had pressed. Louie sank down suddenly on the ground and buried his face in his hands.

Tom and Frank stood over him, in the way a man would try to shield some wounded portion of his own body, instinctively.

A fact obvious to all of them was that their own communication with Earth had been shut off. In this daylight they could not see the observer ship hovering out in space, but its occupants had no doubt seen them, seen what had happened. It, no doubt, was telling Earth what it had seen—the attorney general's office, at any rate. Doubtful that it was including E.H.Q. in its report. Problematical that the attorney general would tell E.H.Q. what had happened.

Cal hoped the observers would have enough sense not to try to land.

12

A second shock, powerfully magnified, hit him then. Because he was personally involved?

For what seemed an interminable time, Cal's mind ceased to function rationally, and like an animal suddenly faced with the unknown he froze, shrank within himself, stood motionless. Yet far down within his mind, there was still detached observation, as if a part of him were removed from all this, still in the role of disinterested observer.

The crew behind him was likewise frozen in tableau. And the colonists in front of him. A balance in number, with himself in between, a still picture from a modernist ballet.

Or a charade. Guess what this is!

He felt laughter bubbling to his lips, recognized it for the beginning of hysteria, and the impulse was washed away.

With that portion of detached curiosity he watched his mind functioning, darting frantically here and there for rational explanation, and momentarily taking refuge in irrationality. It was all being done with trick photography! Such a sudden transition could take place in a motion picture, a transition from reality into a dream sequence lying discarded on the cutting-room floor.

Reversion to the primitive, accounting for the phenomena by devising a mind more powerful than his own. The childhood view of the omnipotent parent, reality's disillusionment, the parent substitute, the creation of a god in his parent's image without the weakness of his parent, so that he might go on in perpetual irresponsibility since he could now place responsibility outside himself.

Or this was a fairy story in which he lived. This was the spell of enchantment. This was magic. And at the first concept of magic, the first lesson of E sharpened into focus once more.

"Anything is magic if you don't understand how it happens, and science if you do."

In that odd, detached portion of his mind he deliberately used the statement as a foundation. Upon it he reconstructed the science of E. The universe and all in it is logical, logical at least to man because he is part of that universe, of its essence. There can be nothing in the universe that is wrong, or out of place, except and only as the limited interpretation of man who sees a force in terms of a threat to the ascendancy of himself-and-his at the center of things. This is the sole basis of morality, and prevents man's appreciation of total reality.

He had been trapped in the first concept, and was accepting these phenomena as a statement of Eminent Authority. But what if this were not the whole of reality, what then?

Once begun, his mind progressed rapidly through the seven stages of E science, and in the seventh he found rationality. If there is only one natural law, and we see it only in seemingly unrelated facets because of our ignorance, because we cannot apperceive the whole, then this, too, is no more than another facet.

Perhaps it was this which broke the spell. Perhaps it was the movement of the colonists. They were moving, withdrawing, walking backward step by step. Their faces were masks of despair, and in them Cal read the knowledge that what had just happened to him, his men, his ship, had previously happened to them.

Slowly they backed away, backed out of the open space, sought the shelter of a great and spreading tree at the edge of the clearing. There they paused.

It was a return to ballet, a gravely executed change in the proportions of the tableau. They stood, a drooped and huddled group, cowering beneath the tree, in nude dejection, in the suggestion of a wary crouch, uncertain whether to flee precipitously, or freeze to make themselves as small and inconspicuous as possible.

In the same grave choreography he turned to look at his crew. And at the turning, as if on signal, on musical cue, Tom and Frank began the pantomime of urging Louie to his feet. Louie looked at the two standing men alternately. With bloodless lips he tried to grin wryly, apologetically, for what his nervous system was doing to his body against his will.

The old flash of an expression which seemed to say, "This is just the kind of dirty trick life always plays on me," came back into his eyes for an instant, and he tried to grin. But the attempt was a grimace of terror. He cowered back down at their feet, his courage swamped in funk.

"Let's get him under the tree," Cal said, and wondered why he had spoken in such a low voice, almost a whisper. That, too, was a part of the classical pattern of fear, to make no noise. As was getting him under the tree, an animal's instinct to hide from the eyes of the unknown.

As the four of them approached the tree, with Tom and Frank half-carrying, half-dragging Louie—and he still trying to make his legs behave, support him—the colonists made a fluttering movement of uncertainty, as if to bolt, to run in panic, farther and farther back into sheltering protection of the deep forest.

But they stood their ground, in acceptance. The seven men came together under the protecting branches of the tree. Protection? From what?

Louie sank down gratefully, and clutched the trunk of the tree, as if, on a high place, he feared falling.

"Sorry," he muttered through clenched teeth. "Just can't help it."

One of the colonists answered first, the tall, leather-faced, spare-framed one. Stamped on his face was his origin, the imperishable impression of the West Texan, grown up in a harsh land that can be made responsive to man's needs only through strength, his will to survive against all odds.

"It figgers," the man said in his quiet drawl. "We've all been like that for days, maybe a week or more. Lost count. You're doin' all right. Better than some."

Cal drew a deep breath, consciously squared his shoulders, sought off the urge to like dejection.

"Then everybody's still alive?" he asked.

"Oh yeah, sure. Nobody's kill't. Just hidin' out in the woods, and mostly from each other. It's a turrible thing." He looked down at himself with a wry grimace. "Not outta shame," he added. "We've seen naked bodies before. Just plumb scared, I guess."

To talk, to hear himself talking, and that to strangers, to tell somebody about it, seemed to restore some confidence in himself. Something of quiet dignity came back over him, a knowledge of responsibility for leadership. He straightened, as if silently reminding himself that he was a man.

"I'm Jed Dawkins," he said. "Sort of the kingpin of the colony, I reckon you might say. Mayor of Appletree, or what was Appletree. I don't rightly know if I'm mayor of anything now. This here is Ahmed Hussein, and this miserable hunk o' man is Dirk Van Tassel. Manner of speakin'," he amended. "He ain't no more miserable than the rest of us."

"I'm Calvin Gray," Cal answered. He indicated his crew. "This is Tom Lynwood, Frank Norton, Louie LeBeau. They're all good men. Just under the weather right now."

"You should'a seen us when it first happened," Jed said with feeling. "I reckon you're the E? Come to find out why we didn't communicate?" He spread his open hands and waved them to indicate the area around him. "Now you see why we didn't.

Hollerin' loud as we could wouldn't do the job, and that's all we got left."

Somehow the introductions relaxed them all a little, as if the familiar formality provided some kind of normalcy in an incredible situation.

"Don't seem right hospitable, just standin' here," Jed added with a shrug. "But there ain't no house, nor camp, nor fire to share with you."

"We're not suffering at the moment, except mentally," Cal reassured him. Involuntarily he glanced up at the spreading branches of the tree, as if to reassure himself also; then grinned in self-consciousness at the pantomime of fear. "First thing is to find out what happened."

"Might as well hunker down right here on the ground," Jed said. "One place is good as another right now."

The men all crouched or sat on the dead leaves which carpeted the ground. Cal suddenly realized he was glad to take the strain from his legs, as if he had been maintaining stance through sheer will.

"It is a poor greeting to visitors from home," Ahmed spoke up, then cleared his voice in surprise to hear himself speaking. "We cannot even provide a cup of coffee."

"Cain't have no fire," Dawkins explained. "See?"

He picked up two dead twigs laying on the ground near him. He began rubbing them together, in the ancient way of creating fire. The two sticks flew apart and out of his hands.

"Try it," he invited Cal.

Curious, even unbelieving, Cal picked up two broken branches. He started to rub them together. He felt them twisted, wrenched, and pulled out of his hands. He saw them flying through the air with a force he had not provided. He got up, picked them up again, sat back down, and held the sticks very tightly in his hands. He tried to bring them together. Suddenly, he simply lost interest.

"Oh to hell with it," he said unexpectedly, and dropped the sticks. His astonishment at himself was a shock.

79

There was a kind of chuckle from Van Tassel, one without mirth. "Kind of gets you, doesn't it?" he said.

Cal looked at his hands, and at the sticks laying beside him. "Now why would I do that?" he asked. "All at once it seemed unimportant to start a fire, or even try. What's happened here? What's been going on?"

"Cain't explain it," Dawkins said. "Sort of hoped you bein' an E, and all. . . ."

"Maybe if you told me just what happened, started at the beginning when everything was normal. . . ."

"Something else you should tell him, Jed," Ahmed spoke up. He looked at Cal, and explained himself. "We don't think easily," he added. "Can't keep our minds on anything for more than a minute or so. In fact, I'm a little surprised that we've been able to carry on the conversation this long. From the way we've been behaving, I would have expected more that we'd have wandered away back into the woods before now—simply left you to your own devices without interest in you. Strange."

"Yeah," Jed confirmed, "I was thinkin' that, too. Funny thing. Right now I feel like I could tell the whole yarn. I feel like. . . . Well, while I'm in the mood I'd better git it said. Don't know how long I can keep interested.

"Well, there we were, one day, seems like it ought to be about a week ago, give or take a couple of days. Anyway, I remember it was around noon. . . ."

13

It was one day around noon.

Jed Dawkins had come in early from his experimental field to get his dinner, well, city folks would call it lunch, and so he'd be ready afterwards for a talk with the colony committee. He'd eaten his lunch, all right, a good one. There was never any scarcity of food on Eden. Always plenty, and wide variety. If anything, a man ate too much and didn't have to work hard enough to get it. That was the main thing that had been wrong with Eden, right from the start. Man was ordained to earn his bread by the sweat of his brow, and there's no reason to sweat for it on Eden.

He was lying on the hammock that was stretched between two big trees in the front yard of his house. The house was set a little way off from the rest of the village, oh maybe five hundred yards more or less, not so far he couldn't be handy when he was needed by the colony, but still far enough to give a man some space.

The domestic sound of rattled pots and pans came from the kitchen window where his wife Martha was washing up after dinner. It was a drowsy, peaceful time. Honeybees they'd brought from Earth were buzzing the flowers Martha had planted all around. A bird was singing up in the trees above him. A man ought to be pretty contented with a life like that, he remembered telling himself. Ought to be.

He felt like taking a nap, but made himself keep awake because the committee was coming right over, and he didn't want to wake up all groggy, the way a man does when he sleeps in the daytime. Couldn't afford to be groggy because the committee was all set up to scrap out something that was splitting the colony right down the middle.

He remembered looking out at the fields where the grains and vegetables were growing, thinking how easy it was to farm here— plenty of rain, plenty of sun, no storms to flatten and ruin the crops, not even enough insect pests to worry a man. He looked out at the fenced pastures where the colony's community stock grazed.

The horses had eaten their fill and were ambling up from the drinking pond, getting ready to take a siesta of their own in the shade of some trees at the corner of their pasture. The cows were already lying down in a grove of trees and were sleepily chewing their cuds. The green grass around them was so tall he could barely see their heads and backs.

His house was on top of a little hill, knoll you might call it. Martha, like himself, had been raised in West Texas where all you could see, as the city feller said, was miles and miles of miles and miles. She never could stand not being able to see a long ways off, and she'd picked out this spot herself. They could see all the valley and the sea, and some dim shapes of islands in the distance. Right nice.

Yes, it was all very peaceful—and tame.

That was the main trouble in the colony. Too tame. Some of them got restless. They argued the five-year test was all right for most planets. You needed every bit of it to prove that man could make it there, or couldn't, or how much help he would need from Earth, maybe for a while, maybe always.

On Eden you didn't have to prove anything. There wasn't anything to make a man feel like a man, proud to be one. Maybe that would be all right for ordinary folks, but for experimental colonists it was a slow death—almost as bad as living on Earth.

Sure, they'd made their complaints to Earth. Half a dozen times or maybe more. They'd asked for an inspector to come out and see for himself, and see what it was doing to the colonists. Jed put it right up to E.H.Q. that they were plumb ruining a prime batch of colonists with this easy living.

A man had to stretch himself once in a while if he expected to grow tall.

Some of the colonists were getting so lazy they'd stopped bitching and were even talking about maybe just staying on here after the experimental was over—maybe getting a doctor to reverse the operation so they could have kids—which, of course, you couldn't have in an experimental colony.

And that was bad. What with easy living and wanting kids as was normal to most, experimental colonists weren't so plentiful that Earth could afford to lose any.

Some of the colonists wanted to leave this—well, they called it a Lotus Land, whatever that was—right away, before everybody went under, got plumb ruined. They were all for taking the escape ship and hightailing it back to Earth. Sure, they knew there'd be a stink, and they'd get a little black mark in somebody's book for not obeying orders to stick it out. But that was better than losing their trade, their desire to follow it. Maybe there'd be a penalty and they'd be marooned to stay on Earth for a while. But they'd bet there was a hundred planets laying idle right now because there weren't enough experimentals to go around.

They'd get a black mark, but after a while they'd get another job too. Anyway, living on Earth couldn't be any worse for them than living here.

Half of them wanted to stay here permanently. The other half wanted to leave right now. That was what the committee was going to decide today. He'd done some checking around, and it looked like they were going to vote to go. He'd also checked with them who wanted to stay permanently, and it looked like, in a showdown, they'd come along. They were proud to be men, too, men and women. Everybody would join. He'd been pretty sure of it.

Even the dissenters who'd moved away across the ridge. That was the trouble with them. There hadn't been enough hardship to bind the community together. People forgot how to be kind to one another and get along when there wasn't any hardship to share among themselves.

It would mean deserting the planet entirely. Even though his sympathies were with the ones who wanted to go, Jed felt there was something wrong, real bad, about deserting the planet. Still and all, if they voted to go he couldn't stop them.

Maybe Earth would let the three-generation colonists come on out without the total test period. But maybe not. Maybe E.H.Q. would decide that Eden was too hard to colonize because it was too easy. Maybe they'd abandon the planet entirely. There'd be no more humans here, and no more coming.

That was when he hit the ground with a solid thump!

He first thought the hammock had somehow twisted out from under him, and he looked up at it resentfully, the way a man blames something else for his own fault. There wasn't any hammock.

At the same time, he heard Martha cry out. He craned his neck quickly in the direction of the house. There wasn't any house. Martha was standing there on bare ground, and there wasn't a dad-blamed thing else, not a stove, nor a chair, a dish, nothing.

And Martha didn't have a stitch of clothes on her!

His first thought was that she ought to have more sense than to stand right out in the yard plumb naked. What was the matter with her anyhow? He peered quickly down toward the village to see if anybody was looking up in this direction.

The whole thing hit him like a blow on top the head. There wasn't any hammock. There wasn't any house.

There wasn't any village.

He saw a whole passel of people squirming around down 'there where the village ought to be. They were standing, or crouched, or lying around as if they'd fallen down.

And every one of the crazy galoots was plumb naked.

And so was he! He'd just realized it.

It had all happened so quietly that that fool bird up in the tree was still singing. Hadn't missed a note. Funny how a thing like that stood out above all the rest. Still singing.

Jed got up on his knees, scrambled to his feet, and dodged behind a tree. Fine lot of authority he'd have as village mayor if anybody saw him standing out in his front yard naked as a jay bird.

The reminder of his responsibility caused him to sweep his eyes beyond the sight of the village to where their spaceship should be in its hangar, always ready for instant escape if anything should go wrong, real wrong, that is. This ship wasn't there. The hangar wasn't there. Nothing.

For a little bit he thought he must be looking in the wrong direction. He'd got turned around or something in the confusion, because there was a grove of trees where the hangar ought to be. And it was the same grove they'd cleared away over two years ago. He recognized one of the trees because it had a peculiar shape.

And he remembered feeding the trunk of that very tree into the power saw for lumber. It was twisted and gnarled, and Martha had asked him to save the wood for furniture because it was real pretty. That was the tree, there on the edge of the grove.

He felt drunk, in a daze. He turned the other direction and looked out where the experimental fields ought to be. They'd cleared that whole area of timber and brush because it was a good, flat land. Only they hadn't, because that was virgin forest, too.

Maybe he'd gone insane? He felt a flood of relief. Sure, that was it. He'd just gone insane, that was all. Everything else was all right.

"The calves have got loose to the cows and they're going to take all the milk, Jed."

He turned around and looked at Martha. If he was crazy, so was she. Her eyes showed it. Her words showed it, at a time like this to be worrying about them fool calves getting out. It took all the comfort away from him. Her face was white, her eyes were dazed.

"You got some dirt on your cheek, Martha," he heard himself saying. "And for Pete's sake, woman, put on some clothes. The committee's coming over, and you running around like that!"

He thought he had the solution then. He'd fallen asleep in the hammock after all, while he was waiting for the committee, and he was dreaming. Of course, he ought to have known all along. This was just the way things happened in a dream—even him and Martha running around naked. He even chuckled to himself. He must be a pretty moral kind of fellow after all, because even in a dream it was his own wife that was next to him there, naked—not some other man's.

The fool things a man can dream! Might as well make the most of it. He took her into his arms, and she clung to him.

Must have got the sheet tangled around his throat to choke him, and he was dreaming it was her arms. But there hadn't been any sheet in the hammock when he went to sleep.

And he wasn't dreaming.

"What's happened, Jed?" she whispered. Even her whisper was shaking with fear, and her arms were wound around his neck so tight now he could hardly breathe.

"Now, now, Martha," he cautioned. "Don't you go getting hysterical."

"What has happened?" she asked again.

"I don't know," he said. They were both talking in low tones.

"It's some kind of a miracle," she whispered.

"Now there's a woman's thinking for you," he chided her fondly, joshing her a little. "Nothing of the sort. It's just plain . . . Well any scientist would tell you that. . . ." And then he stopped.

He was pretty sure the frameworks of science, as he knew them, wouldn't be able to tell you.

He guessed that while they stood there clinging to one another, they both went a little nuts. It was sort of like drowning, he guessed. You'd have the feeling of sinking down and down, and there'd be nothing but blinding, swirling chaos all around you. Then you'd kind of come to for a minute, and there'd be the trees, the sky, the farm animals, the sea in the distance.

You'd look down toward the village, and make a mental note, almost absently, that people were getting to their feet now, some of them clinging together the way you and Martha were—and then back down into mental chaos you'd go again.

That went on several times, he remembered, before he'd begun to snap out of it a little.

"But the funniest thing of all," Jed said, and looked at Cal quickly, penetratingly. "I had the feeling all the time that we were being watched!"

Cal said nothing.

"You know," Jed explained. "Like catching an animal in a trap? Then watching it, to see what it will do?"

Cal nodded, without speaking.

"It was just another crazy thought, I guess," Jed said deprecatingly. "Plumb crazy."

But, clearly, he didn't believe it was.

14

At E.H.Q. on Earth communication had been working fine. The operator sat back and listened with trained ear alert for flaw or fade. A glance at the adjacent recording instrument told him it was taking down everything said—had been for hours.

Nice deal about those naked colonists. Maybe the astronavigator on the E cruiser had been right. Maybe they'd all just gone back to nature, all the way back.

He wondered if there were any pretty young female colonists. And how far did that word experimental take you? Some experiment! He realized his interest was running deeper than that of a detached technician's concern for well-operated equipment—mechanical, that is. Well, let it. Live a little once in a while. At least dream.

The department supervisor hovered near the back of the operator's chair, breathing down his neck. He gnawed at the knuckles of his hand, and hoped nothing would go wrong this time. That astronavigator, Louie LeBeau, was probably right. Those colonists had turned nudist, and were afraid to report what they'd done back to Earth!

Well!

He looked around guiltily, wondering if he'd exclaimed it aloud. He decided he hadn't.

If *he* were out there, instead of that E, *he'd* make them put their clothes back on, on the double. Getting everything all upset, causing all this trouble, getting everybody excited, all of E.H.Q. aroused, taking up the time of an E—just because they wanted to frolic around without any clothes on!

If they were going to act like irresponsible children, they should be spanked like irresponsible children.

He wondered if there were any young pretty female colonists who ought to be spanked.

". . . E Gray has just stepped off the landing ramp," the pilot out there was reporting. "He is walking toward the three colonists. Now they have started walking toward him. They do not seem hostile. They seem glad to see us. My crew and I are still at our stations, ready for. . . ."

Silence.

The set simply didn't register anything more except that faint sigh of uncompleted force fields in space.

"What now? What now?" the supervisor pushed the operator to one side, and barely restrained the impulse to cuff him on the side of the head. "Now what did you do? Why did you meddle with it when it was coming in so clear and strong? What's happened?"

"I didn't do anything. I didn't meddle with it. I don't know what's happened," the operator flared back. "The signal just stopped. That's all."

There was an imperative flashing of the signal light on the line that had been rigged to give direct connection of the running report to Hayes's office. The operator hesitated, then flipped open the key, as if he were touching a rattlesnake.

"What's happened down there?" Hayes complained abruptly, without diplomatic softness. "This is a very crucial point!"

"I don't know what happened. I don't know," the supervisor quarreled back. "The signal just stopped coming. We weren't doing anything to the equipment."

He looked up at the continuously changing tri-di star map which made the far wall appear to be a view into a miniature universe. "There's no reason for an occlusion," he said to Hayes. "And the set here is alive. It must be at the other end."

He turned to the operator, and said loudly, "Bounce a beam on Eden's surface. Just see if any booster has gone out between here and there." Most of it was making a show of efficiency for Hayes.

"Here we go again," the operator mumbled to himself, and pressed down a key. The returning pips showed the signal was getting through to Eden.

"Pilot Lynwood! Pilot Lynwood!" the supervisor nagged into the mike. "Speak up! Do you hear me?"

The operator sighed deeply. His panel partner grimaced something halfway between a grin and a sneer of disgust.

"They don't answer," the supervisor said at last to Hayes. "It's the same as before."

"Here we go again," Hayes groaned, but not only to himself. "All right," he said wearily, after a moment's hesitation. "Keep the channel open. Keep trying to contact them. Let me know if signal resumes."

But he already felt the conviction that it would do no good. It was too much of the same pattern as before. What could have happened?

There'd have to be another review, he supposed. A longer and more detailed one. There must be, had to be, something they'd overlooked in the first one. Had he been right in freezing out so many who wanted to speculate in that first one? But in the interests of time!

The scientists would grumble, even worse than before, because now each one of them would be worried lest it was his own field of knowledge that had failed. Hunting a needle in a haystack was easy. At least you knew what a needle looked like, could recognize it when you saw it.

It would probably all end with nothing solved. E McGinnis would go out in a rescue ship. He'd already told E Gray that he would be available in an emergency, and this looked like an emergency. And that would leave E.H.Q. without a single E in residence.

Why didn't General Administration get busy and qualify more E's? It shouldn't be so difficult as all that to teach people to think! There was something mighty wrong with the way kids were brought up if only one in a million could still think by the time he was grown. Less than one in a million could qualify as an E.

A boy had to be a natural rebel to start with, because if he believed what people said he wouldn't get anywhere, no farther than the people who said it. And if he didn't believe what they told him, they punished him, outcast him, whipped him, violenced him into submission if they could. If they couldn't they shut him up in a prison, labeled him dangerous to society.

It was a wonder that any were able to walk the thin line between rebelliousness and delinquency! And if a few were able, they were still of no use unless they learned what science had to offer as a base. Ah, there was the rub. How to keep alive the curiosity, the inquisitiveness, the skepticism; and at the same time teach him the basics he must have for constructive thought? For if he were not beaten into submission by the punitive methods of society, he was persuaded into it by his teachers, who were ever so sure of their facts and proofs.

Now you take this Eden problem. Probably wouldn't be tough at all if a guy could just think. But what could have happened?

He understood there was an observer ship out there, sent out by the attorney general's office. Why wasn't it reporting? Probably was—to the attorney general's office. Fine lot of good E.H.Q. would get out of that. He was no fool. He knew the attorney general would gladly sacrifice the whole lot of colonists, if it would give him a weapon to fight E.H.Q.

Why hadn't E.H.Q. sent along an observer ship also? These cocky E's! Probably hadn't thought it necessary. Always ready to assume they could handle the situation by themselves!

He wondered if he dared voice that criticism during the review, get it on record. He thought about it, and decided in favor of playing it safe. Maybe that was the trouble. Everybody was too concerned with his own skin, too willing to play it safe. But an employee of E.H.Q. to make a public criticism of an E! No, better play it safe.

He sighed heavily, and asked the operator to please see if E McGinnis would talk to him.

He suspected that E McGinnis would just stand off from the planet and wait for E Gray to get in touch. Nothing seemed to have happened while E Gray's cruiser was out in space. It must be something connected with landing, being on the surface of the planet.

But E Gray could signal to E McGinnis. Those pesky colonists! Why hadn't they signaled to E Gray? Why hadn't they come out of their bushes and signaled the danger? Surely they must know what it was. They were alive and healthy, three of them at least. Why hadn't they used their stupid heads?

But then, how could they have known E Gray was out in space, or even in their stratosphere? Well, they had telescopes, didn't they? Or did they? Sure they did. No matter what happened to the buildings, they must have all sorts of equipment hidden under the trees, or in caves.

Why hadn't E Gray been more cautious about landing? Rushing in there like a green school kid, without even rudimentary precautions. That's what came from sending out a boy to do a man's job. Maybe the attorney general's office had been right in its attempt to prevent a junior from going. What was the use of all that E training, if the boy didn't have enough sense. . . .

At least E McGinnis would have enough sense to stand off, not go rushing in blindly. Grand old man, E McGinnis. Now there was a *real* product of E science, the veritable dean of the E's.

E Gray would probably have enough sense to know he'd be followed by a rescue ship as soon as something went wrong. And between an E out in space and another on the ground, they shouldn't have any trouble in working it out. He wondered if he should suggest that to E McGinnis as soon as the operator located him. Even if the grand, lovable old man thought of it for himself, he'd compliment Hayes for thinking it, reasoning it all out!

The intercom operator came on his line.

"Sir," she said, and cleared her throat. He could hear her gulp. Her voice was very small, thin. "Sir," she began again. "I contacted E McGinnis. He said some things. He told me to tell you exactly what he said, word for word. I took it down in shorthand, so I could."

"Well! Well!" he exclaimed impatiently. His brusqueness seemed to give her courage.

"Sir," she said a little stronger. "E McGinnis won't talk to you. He says the foggy, rambling way that review was conducted was a disgrace. He says why don't you get on with what you have to do instead of bothering people. He says not to waste any more of his time unless you can come up with something he doesn't already know. He says he doubts you'd know what that was even if it hit you in the face. He said to tell you the exact words, so I took it down in shorthand, so I could. Because—he said to."

She was all but wailing, as she finished.

"All right," Hayes sighed tiredly. Senile old devil! No wonder things were going to pot, if this was a sample of E training. "Send me your notes so I can follow them carefully," he told the operator.

"So you can tear them up before they get spread all over the joint," she mumbled, but she had already thrown the key so he couldn't hear her.

Resignedly, because he knew he was going to catch it from the scientists just as bad, because he was feeling very sorry for himself that he must always be in the middle of things, he began to arouse the scientists.

He felt so sorry for himself that he dropped his tentative plan to have the midgit-idgit check the personal attributes of the individual colonists out there—to see if some of them might be young, pretty, female—34-24-34.

As if the idea were now red hot, he dropped the plan of telling General Administration that, since Eden was in his sector, perhaps he should go out there, personally.

15

The observer ship, with an assistant attorney general aboard was, indeed, reporting directly to the attorney general's office—to Gunderson in person. On their own secret channel, of course. Had to be secret. All right for them to know, because they were very special persons, but the people should not be told.

"Gray is coming out of the ship," the assistant was saying. "He is starting down the ramp. He is alone. He has no apparent weapons. Making a grandstand play of it. Far as we can tell, the crew isn't covering him. Now he is at the foot of the ramp. The three unclothed men are moving toward him, spread out a little, crouching, obviously going to attack. The stupid fool doesn't seem to realize it. He's. . . .

"Wait a minute. I don't believe it. . . ."

"Well, what?" Gunderson exploded from his end.

"Sir," the assistant gulped, "the ship disappeared, just like that."

"Nonsense!"

"No sir. It did. The three crewmen are sprawled on the ground. Now two of them are getting up. There isn't a sign of the ship, the ramp, or anything."

"Can't be. Has to be around somewhere."

"No sir. Isn't. Sorry to contradict you, sir. It isn't anywhere."

"They probably set controls to send the ship back into space, and jumped out before it took off. Search space. You'll find it. Ships don't just disappear."

"I'll search, of course. But this ship just disappeared."

"All right, what's going on? What else?"

"They're naked. Naked as the day they were born. All four of them. Same as the colonists."

"Keep track of where they put their clothes. Photograph it. Get the evidence."

"Sir, their clothes disappeared right off their bodies. First they were fully dressed, Gray was, anyhow. Maybe the crew could have undressed inside the ship, but Gray was fully dressed—and then he wasn't. Just like that."

"Hm-m."

"Shall I land, sir? Place them under arrest?"

"Wait a minute. Let's think of a good charge. Something to stand up in court. Have to make this airtight right from the beginning in case some stupid judge decides to make a show of independence."

"Indecent exposure, sir? Lewd public behavior?"

"Pretty weak, in view of what's involved."

"A suggestion, sir. Maybe a morals charge is the most effective weapon we could have. Attack the E structure on the grounds of bad scientific judgment, and every egghead on Earth will feel compelled to rise up in their defense—except, of course, those employed by the government. But on a morals charge there wouldn't be one voice raised—fear of being tarred with the same brush. Except maybe a few radicals that are already discredited. Any other charge might get public sentiment aroused against us, but a morals charge—think of the backing we'd get from the women's clubs, P.T.A., all the pressure groups determined to dictate to the rest of the world how it should behave. It's worked for hundreds of years, sir. Never fails."

"Hm-m," Gunderson mused. "You may be right."

"Shall I land, sir, make the arrest?"

"You've got plenty of photographic evidence?"

"All we'd need, sir, at least for the lewd, public indecent exposure charge."

"Wait a minute. How about the colonists? Got pictures of them?"

"The three men, sir. No others."

"Let's don't rush into this," Gunderson said slowly. "Without a ship they're not going to get far. Hold off, and keep taking pictures. Maybe we can get something stronger on Gray than just an indecent exposure, or at least get some pictures that could be interpreted as more than just that. Get pictures of as many colonists as possible, too, in case they've gone nudist."

"You'd want to prosecute the colonists, too?"

"Might be a smart idea. That way, nobody could claim we'd been gunning for the junior E. Make it impartial, play no favorites. Hm-m, even if we decided not to prosecute, we'd have the pictures in their dossiers, so that anytime in the future, for the rest of their lives, if any of them gave us any trouble, we could quietly let them know what we've got, and they'll just fold up and quit. That's worked for hundreds of years, too."

"Yes, sir. Smart thinking, sir." The assistant knew that already Gunderson had adopted the idea as his own, and to hold his job he'd better let Gunderson go on thinking so. Of course, if the idea should backfire, then Gunderson would remember quickly enough where it had originated.

"Hm-m, you know," Gunderson was saying. "This could work out all right. If their ship's gone they're not communicating with E.H.Q. And if they're not communicating, E.H.Q. will send out another ship to see why. Maybe there'll be an E on it. I hear the only one available is McGinnis—that guy who's planning to fight us on that injunction.

"Now suppose he landed. Suppose he went nudist, or we could make pictures look like he did. The guy would have to undress sometime, take a bath. Slap a morals charge on him. Nobody with a public reputation ever fights a charge like that, guilty or innocent. They pay up or knuckle under to keep it quiet. Have, for hundreds of years; always will, as long as a bunch of fat, old, ugly biddies, male and female, who nobody wants that way are viciously resentful that they can't have what somebody else is enjoying. Young ones, too, so twisted and warped with frustrations they don't dare try what they daydream about. They're even worse. Yeah, a morals charge is the way to get at him."

"But I understood there was a law, that we couldn't charge an E for any offense."

"We can try him in the newspapers, can't we? On the televiewers. That's the whole point. We can't charge an E now, but wait until we get things stirred up on a morals basis. That law'll be changed in a hurry, because any legislator that tried to hold out against changing it would be drawn and quartered by his constituents—and has enough sense to know it.

"Hm-m," he breathed in satisfaction. "That's the way to go about it. Don't know why I haven't thought of it before. If you guys would read your history of how police enforcement officers got things back under control each time some idealist started squawking about human rights, you'd think of these things, too.

"Now don't go off half-cocked. Just stand by. Keep me posted on every move. If I've got to do the thinking on how to get those E's back under police control, the way scientists were before, I've got to have information.

"And keep taking pictures!"

16

"After everything disappeared, the buildings, the escape ship, everything," Cal reviewed, "and you, with your wife, found yourself crouching under the trees in what had been your front yard, without any clothes on—what then?"

"That was the beginning of it," Jed Dawkins answered. He looked toward his two companions as if for confirmation. He looked at the three crewmen, at Cal, all sprawled or crouched there beneath the tree at the edge of the clearing. "We thought it was the end of everything," he said in retrospect, "but we found out quick that things had just begun."

Cal nodded. Dawkins had told his tale simply, without fictitious emotionalism, without straining to get the horror of it across— and thereby succeeded. He glanced at his three crewmen, to see how they were faring. Louie, seemed to have gained some control over his nerves, and yet the way he sat there staring at nothing showed he was enduring some special horror of his own. Frank Norton shifted his position, pulled a dry stick from beneath the leaves, looked at it resentfully, and tossed it aside. He settled back down and indicated by his expression that now he could be more comfortable.

One grateful fact, the day was warm, the breeze under the tree was gentle, the ground on which they sat was not too wet for comfort. Except for custom, for modesty, clothes weren't really needed; and perhaps the shock of being without them would pass. Nudists, on Earth, claimed that one very quickly lost all self-consciousness if no one were clothed; that such was part of the value; that sex, for instance, became less of an issue instead of more because, without concealment, one could see instead of imagining, and the sight more often discouraged then enticed. Cal wondered what the militant moralists would make of the idea that clothes encouraged immorality.

"It was a hard thing to believe," Jed was saying. "It wasn't like a natural thing—like a cyclone, or earthquake, or fire, or flood. Nothin' like that. Them things a man can understand. Even if he's dyin', at least he knows, he understands, what's killin' him. I never thought I'd hear myself say it would be a comfort to know what you was dyin' of, but, believe me. . . ."

He broke off and stared in front of himself. His voice took on a note of perplexity.

"Only nobody died. Nobody even got hurt. We was like little kids screamin' at the top of their lungs when they ain't hurt at all—only scared." He looked abashed. "I got to tell you, real truthful," he said, "most of the yellin' came from the men. The women, by and large, was real swell.

"Fact is," he continued, "come to think of it, I don't recollect ever seein' a woman in real hysterics. Plenty of fake, of course. Say she's tryin' to hook some man into protectin' her; or lay public blame on him for not doin' it. Other times, in real danger, womenfolks, our kind of womenfolks, anyhow, they pitch right in and help. It takes a man to make a jackass outta himself at the wrong time."

Cal nodded and smiled. There was an attempt at a hollow laugh from Louie, as if the shoe had fit. Jed didn't seem to realize it, and made no apology about present company being excepted.

"It wasn't like the aftermath of a storm, either," Jed said, "where you begin pickin' up the pieces to start over. We—we couldn't pick up any pieces."

They couldn't pick up any pieces. In a way, that was worse than the disappearance of things. In a catastrophe, after taking care of those that are hurt, first thing a man does is gather the materials and tools to fix things up again. The women, after soothing them that's hurt, taking care of them as much as possible, first thing they think of is making hot coffee, maybe hot soup.

That was when they began to realize this was more than the desolation following a cyclone or other freak of nature.

Cal wanted to know what happened? Well, there he was, still sort of hiding behind his tree. It was Martha who snapped out of it first, who insisted that clothes or no clothes it was their plain duty to get down to the village where they could help somebody. He'd need other men to help him get things back in shape; she could help the other women take care of the needy.

And still he hung back, ashamed of his nakedness. She scolded him then, pointed out that if everybody was naked, their being naked too wasn't likely to start up a passel of gossip.

He gave in to her scolding, because she was right, and came out from behind his tree. It seemed more than passing strange to be walking down that slope naked, in plain sight of everybody. Thing that helped was that nobody seemed of a mind to stop and stare at them.

Everybody had his mind on his own problems, and then a funny thing happened. Maybe, Jed reasoned, it was seeing that everybody else was naked too. Anyway, the self-consciousness disappeared all of a sudden, and they didn't think any more about it—not right then, anyhow.

By the time they'd got to the foot of their hill and into the crowd of people, he forgot all about it. There was plenty of other things to think about. Martha pitched right in, the way he ought to have done. She was the one who thought of giving the men something to do, get them over their hysterics.

"Why don't some of you men get a fire going!" she called out, as soon as they got to the edge of the crowd. "Something hot to drink is what we need most. Hot water, in case anybody is hurt."

Of course she wasn't thinking straight, not entirely. They didn't have a pot to heat water in. Or maybe she was, because right away he heard her asking other women if any of them knew where there might be some dried gourds. He remembered then an old pioneer trick—cutting open a gourd, scooping out the seed, filling it with water, dropping hot stones into it until it boiled, Indian style.

It might seem funny to city women, always protected against everything, that Martha wasn't more excited, and helpless. First place, she had her man already, and didn't need to put on such a show. Second place, she was a colonist woman, an experimental colonist woman, trained all her life to take care of the unexpected; and for the experimentals something unexpected was always happening.

Under her influence, and maybe a little under his, Jed acknowledged, now that he'd been set straight by Martha's example, everybody began to settle down a little, like they would after the first shock of a fire or flood. It was all over. Now it was time to start picking up the pieces, rebuilding.

Only it wasn't all over.

That's when they found out they couldn't build a fire.

Easiest way, without matches, is to string a bow and twirl a stick in a hole punched into another stick. Next easiest way is to find a piece of flint, strike two pieces together to make sparks and hope one will set a wad of punk on fire. If no other way, rubbing two dry sticks together will do it if you can rub them fast enough, get them hot enough to make the powdered fibers burst into flame. Or if they'd had some of those quartz crystals from the top of the mountain to focus sun rays. . . .

But they couldn't make a bow, or strike two stones together, or rub two sticks together. It couldn't be done. Well, Cal had seen for himself what happened when it was tried. All the men were trying it, and for a little bit everybody thought it was only happening to him, that he must have lost the knack, or something. For a little bit there the men were more worried about how their wife would bring it up for weeks or months, how he had let the rest of the men show him up when it came to building a fire.

One of the men tore it then.

He yelled out that somebody he couldn't see was watching him over his shoulder, that it wasn't meant they should have fire.

Cal looked quickly at Louie at that point of the story. Louie was staring, with mouth open, at Jed; and in his eyes was confirmation of that same feeling. But Jed didn't notice the effect, and went on with the telling.

Everybody stopped and listened to the man, because they were having the same feeling. Jed knew it. Him, too. The crowd might have panicked right there if the man had let it rest, but he started explaining it, the way a man does, and makes himself ridiculous.

He kept on yelling how the men shouldn't listen to the women. That it was in the first Garden of Eden that man had made the mistake of listening to woman; that it was Eve who had egged Adam into eating that apple because a woman was never satisfied to leave well enough alone. And now, he said, in this new Eden, man was being given another chance. If he was smart, if he's learned anything at all, this time he wouldn't listen to no woman.

Somebody bust out laughing when he said that, and it kind of eased the tension a little.

A woman said, real disgusted, that if the men was too helpless to start a little fire, least they could do was scrape up some dry leaves because in a few hours it would get dark. Magic or no magic, watchers or no watchers, night would fall, and she for one liked a soft bed. That caused them to look up at the sky, and sure enough the sun, Ceti, was already half way down the sky from where it had been at noon. At least the world was turning and time was moving. That, at least. About three hours had passed in what seemed like minutes.

Somebody else, one of the men this time, said why didn't they go a little farther than scraping up some leaves. Why didn't they get busy and knock together some shelters in case it rained during the night—the way it often did.

Now any one of them, man or woman, ought to have been able to put up a small shelter in less time than it takes to tell about it, even without no tools. Break off a limb, or take a sharp stone, dig holes in the ground with it. Take straight saplings, trim them, stick them upright in the ground, tamp in the dirt good and hard, lash them together with vines, lash other poles together to make the frame of the roof, lift that onto the poles and lash them all together with braces. Thatch it with grass, and there you were.

But there they weren't. They couldn't do it.

Things just wouldn't behave. They dug a hole, and it filled right up again. They couldn't cut down a sapling, because the sharp stone, the only tool they had, would fly out of their hands. They even tried lashing some saplings together where they grew, and the saplings were like things alive. They wouldn't be bound. The vines slithered out of their hands and dropped to the ground, and the saplings sprang up again straight.

Not only that. They could scrape together some leaves into a pile, all right, but when anybody tried to lie down in them the leaves would scatter as if blown by a wind. Only there wasn't any wind.

Some of the women got pretty disgusted with their menfolks. They tried it themselves, and the same things happened. After that, they was a little more forgiving.

A couple more hours had passed while they were trying that. The sun got low. People began to realize they were getting hungry, and they began to realize there wasn't any way to cook supper.

Now there wasn't any real hardship, not physical. Nobody'd been hurt. Shook up a little, scared for sure. But not hurt.

The river was still flowing good, clean water. All they had to do was go down to the river bank and cup the water in their hands, lift it to their lips; or even better, lie down on the bank and lower their faces into the water. They could do that. It helped a little to know they could.

The wild bushes and trees all around had plenty of fruit and nuts to eat. One thing you could say for Eden, the fruit didn't seem to depend on seasons. There was always something ripe, and plenty of it.

The people wandered off from the village site then, to forage their supper, for all the world like animals grazing in a pasture. They sort of hung together, in herds, glad to be together—then.

By dark they all came back and sat around in a circle, the way people in the wilds sit around a campfire. It seemed funny without a campfire. The darker it got, the funnier it felt. The more you thought about it, the stranger it got. The excitement had begun to wear off, and people were starting to think a little. It got stranger and stranger. In the dusk you could see the same thought in all the gleaming eyes.

They couldn't have fire!

Maybe the strangest thing of all, nobody was trying to explain what had happened. Now you take mankind, he's always right in there with an explanation for everything. Maybe it's not the right one, maybe, looking back, it's a silly one—but at the time he believes it, and that's a comfort.

But this was like being in a dream, knowing it's a dream, knowing it can't happen this way, and so it doesn't have to be explained. And yet, isn't that the worst part of a bad dream? No explanation for what's happening in it? Nothing you can do about it, either?

Somebody said, it being dark and all, they should get some sleep. Somebody mentioned being thankful there weren't any children. That was one of the hardships of being an experimental colonist, you couldn't have children. Wouldn't be right to expose children to hardships they'd have to suffer helpless. Only here, the way kids were, he wouldn't have been surprised if kids would have taken to it a lot easier than the grown folks.

The people sort of bedded down all together, the way a herd of animals take shelter, each, even in its sleep, taking comfort from the presence and protection of the others. They bedded around on the ground, making themselves comfortable as possible. One thing you could say, experimental colonists might not be long on brains, the way scientists are, but they weren't picked for that.

They were picked for endurance, and the brainy will often crack up under a strain that the enduring kind hardly notices. Far as endurance went, physical, this wasn't bad.

Up through the leaves, and in between the trees, the stars were as bright as ever—brighter because there wasn't no fire to dim their glow. They couldn't see Earth, of course, but everybody knew right where to look for Sol. There it was, a tiny little spot of light in its constellation. It was still there.

Somebody said into the darkness that it was only two more days until the regular monthly communication with Earth was due. That as soon as E.H.Q. didn't hear from them, there'd be a rescue party out here in nothing flat. So, at worst, it meant living this way only five or six more days.

That made everybody feel better. It was a comforting thing to look up through the leaves, to see Sol in the sky, to know they weren't forgotten back home; that on Earth people would soon be buzzing around like a disturbed hive of hornets, with stingers cocked and ready as soon as the message didn't get through.

Yep, somebody said, just like the museum collection of Western movies where the U.S. cavalry always got there in time. At least they weren't being attacked by no Indians, somebody said.

Or were they? Maybe everybody asked that to themselves, but nobody said it.

Most everybody got some sleep. No one really suffered, any discomfort just showed them how soft they were getting with easy living. Considering everything, they were coming along just fine. And in a few days everything would be all right again. They went to sleep thinking that even if there was some equivalent to the old-time Indians attacking them, rescue would soon be here and they would be safe.

Because man always wins.

Most people were wide awake by dawn. Some had slept in little bits, waking often enough to keep a sense of continuity. Others, those who slept better, awoke with a start; looked around themselves wildly, realized they were lying out in the open plumb naked in front of other people; maybe wondered for an instant what kind of party they'd been to the night before; and nearly bolted in panic before they remembered.

Most everyone felt sort of surprised that things weren't back to normal, with yesterday being something soonest forgot soonest mended. It takes time for folks to realize—things.

Not having a hot drink for breakfast was another little hardship, a reminder of how soft they'd got. But nobody complained. Seemed like everybody had woke with a determination to make the best of things and help one another do the same. Everybody was pitching in together to make the best of things. Once they bit into the cool fruit on the trees around them, even not having a hot drink to start the day didn't seem to matter.

Some of the women got together and decided it would help things get back to normal if the people covered their nakedness, or least parts of it. It might be all right just among themselves, they said, because everybody was in the same fix and knew what happened—but how would they feel when the rescue ship landed and they had to walk out in front of strange men with nothing on?

They picked some big green leaves without any trouble. But when they strove to pin them together with thorns, the thorns just slipped out and fell to the ground. Then they tried sewing the leaves together with bindweed. Same thing. The bindweed slithered out and fell to the ground.

One woman figured to stick some leaves together with thick mud from the river and paste them with more mud on her body. It wouldn't stick, peeled right off like she was oiled. One man said he could do it without leaves, just cover himself with mud. He lay down in a muddy pool and got himself covered with wet clay.

He was a sight. All at once he looked vulgar, obscene. And nobody had, before. That did it. Somebody said they were humans, not pigs, and if the men on the rescue ship had never seen a naked body before it was time they did. What was so wrong about the human body, anyhow?

They made the muddy man go bathe himself in the river, and gave up trying to cover themselves. All at once the desire to cover themselves was a nasty kind of thinking, something to be ashamed of.

Midmorning somebody got to wondering if the ten colonists who'd broken off from the main colony and moved across the ridge were all right.

Soon as he reminded them, everybody began to laugh. What fools they'd all been. Showed you how a bit of trouble could keep a man from thinking straight. Here they'd been eating and sleeping like animals when, all the while, just across the ridge there'd be houses and beds, fires and clothes. Sure, those folks might differ in some opinions, but humans always stood ready to help one another in distress, differences forgotten.

In a body, they started for the ridge. Everybody knew just where the dissidents had built their homes. But when they got to the top of the ridge there weren't no houses there. Nothing but virgin woods, same as this side. That shook them up. They'd been so sure.

Maybe it was the jolt of that, maybe it was a measure that we still weren't thinking straight, something—they didn't go on down and join forces. Nobody thought of it, somehow. They went back down and congregated around where the village had been. Maybe it was the beginning of something that would come later, something Cal would see for himself. That they were already not thinking the way humans do. Thinking and behaving more the way dumb animals do.

Nothing else worth mentioning happened that day, nor the next. In some ways it was still like a dream. The way people were just accepting things, without question, maybe without curiosity. Jed remembered one time an E had said there was a wider gap between the thinking man and the average man than there was between that average man and the ape. He'd resented it at the time, of course, but now he thought of it again and began to realize what the E had meant.

Two or three people commented on how easy it was to go back to nature, wondered why they hadn't all done it before. How stupid it was for man to knock himself out chasing all over the universe, undergoing such hardships, when all a man could ever want was right here.

Jed tried to put down this kind of talk when it came up. He reminded them it was Lotus Land thinking, and would be the ruination of a prime bunch of colonists. He reminded them they'd been through hardships worse than this, and had ought to keep their wits about them.

Funny thing, though. He couldn't get very excited about it. Just did it because it was his duty. Maybe not even that strong, maybe because once upon a time, long ago, hardly remembered, it had been his duty.

It was the next day that things got real rough.

Somebody, in a clearer-thinking moment, said they couldn't be sure when the rescue ship would get here; that when the rescuers came and didn't see any village they wouldn't know what to think—maybe they'd just go away. Shows we weren't thinking so straight after all, to believe that you'd go away just because you didn't find our village.

Anyhow, hadn't we ought to work out some kind of a message? Maybe scrape some kind of a message on the ground? They decided the smooth sand above the tide line down on the sea shore was the best place for it.

Nobody had anything else to do, so the whole colony, all forty of them, walked the couple of miles down to the seashore. They picked out a nice stretch of white sand, and with a broken piece of driftwood they started to scratch a message, just a big SOS. The driftwood wriggled out of their hands like a snake. Nobody could hold it. Several men tried together, made no difference.

Somebody started scooping out a furrow with his hands. The

furrow closed up and smoothed out right behind him. Somebody tried piling up sand, first in letters, then in code signals. Made no difference. Sand smoothed right out again.

Then somebody got a bright idea. All right, he said. Didn't need to use a stick, or scoop out a furrow, or pile up the sand. They had their bare feet, didn't they? They could tromp out the letters that way. Footprints, close together, would be as good as a furrow.

That's when it happened.

Jed tried it himself. And his footprints disappeared. They just weren't there. Everybody looked behind himself, where he'd been walking. Nobody was leaving any footprints.

That's when they bolted in panic.

17

Jed looked quickly at Cal when he told him how the colonists had spooked, bolted in panic. As if he expected disbelief.

"Maybe that seems funny to you," he commented. "After taking so much we'd spook like crazy animals and hightail for the woods over not making footprints."

"Pretty fundamental thing," Cal said with a shrug. "Animals are aware of spoor long before they are aware of tools. It hit deep down into fundamental being, a thing like that."

Jed looked relieved. Hussein and Van Tassel exchanged glances, as if confirming their belief that an E would understand their problems. Cal appreciated the confidence expressed in that glance, but did not feel it was justified. It was now pretty obvious that this was some alien co-ordinate system, never before encountered by man. But how to get hold of it? How to reconcile with it? Coexist with it?

Never before encountered by man? What if the myths of early man be true? And too authentic the legends of his being a pawn to the will of the gods? Could there have been some factual basis for the gods? And not, as was supposed, rationalizations dreamed up by man to account for the control of phenomena at a level beyond his own power to control?

"It's been bad since then," Jed continued. "Seems like once they got the wind up, the whole thing hit them all over again. Like cattle in a stampede, they didn't have a lick of sense. They didn't even stay together. They scattered in all directions, hid out in the bushes from each other.

"You could hunt for 'em, call for 'em, yell your lungs out. You could pass within ten feet of one of 'em, callin', pleadin', and they wouldn't say a word. Just stand there and watch you like a hunted animal, not even breathin' lest you discover them.

"After a couple of days, some of us kind of pulled ourselves together—me and Martha, Ahmed and Dirk here. Maybe a dozen of us now have got together again. Funny thing though, even so, all we want is to hide. Can't get over hidin', somehow. That's why you didn't see us from the air. We was hidin' from you.

"Martha, couple other womenfolks, they practically had to push us out of the woods to come greet you, lead you to us. They wouldn't come themselves, being naked and all. They told us, first thing was to get some clothes for them from the ship.

"We was countin' on the arrival of your ship to bring the rest of the colonists back to their senses. Some ain't been found yet, not since the footprint thing. If they were watchin' you from hidin' places, if they also saw your ship disappear—well now, I just don't know."

"There'll be another ship from Earth," Cal said. "In a matter of fifteen or twenty hours at most. We were communicating at the time. They'll know we didn't cut out through choice."

"Yes," Tom Lynwood confirmed. "As I remember, I got cut off in the middle of a sentence. They'll know something was wrong."

"There's another ship out there right now," Cal added. "Not an E.H.Q. ship, but one that would have seen what happened. We'll not count on anything from them, but an E.H.Q. ship will be here soon, probably with an E on board—McGinnis."

"Don't know what good it would do," Jed said despondently. "That ship might disappear, too, soon as it landed. And the next, and the next."

"I don't plan to let it land," Cal told them. "You'll notice nothing happened to us until we touched ground. I'll find a way to talk to the ship, keep it from landing until we've got a line on whatever this is."

"You figger to solve this one?" Jed asked curiously, unbelieving.

"I'm going to try," Cal said with more confidence than he felt. "It's what I'm here for. Maybe I can't solve it, but I can try."

"I don't know how you're going to start," Dirk spoke up. "We're just like animals here. We can't use tools."

"But animals do use tools," Cal answered after a moment. "Materials, anyway. Birds build nests using sticks, grass, clay. Monkeys and apes throw sticks and stones. Even insects use materials. Basic difference between man and the rest is that man gives special shapes to tools, where mainly the rest use whatever falls to hand. But all higher, organized protoplasmic life uses tools in one form or another."

"We ain't allowed to," Jed said emphatically. "Not even what's at hand. Somebody, or somethin', is bound and determined we ain't goin' to."

At that moment Cal felt close to a solution, or at least an understanding of the nature of the problem, which is the first step toward solution. But like the specter seen in twilight from the corner of the eye, as soon as he tried to focus on the problem, the concept disappeared. Something about protoplasmic life using materials. Non-protoplasmic life? Could there be, and still meet the definitions of what constitute life? As compared with our evolution, from its earliest beginning finding some other approach to the manipulation of the physical universe? A totally alien kind of science? Come to think of it, the use of material to affect other material was a cumbersome, indirect, awkward way of going about it, as compared with. . . .

Compared with what?

The concept would not yet allow him full focus upon it. He filed it away for future contemplation.

He saw Dawkins and the other colonists looking at him defiantly, as if interpreting his silence to be doubt of their veracity about the taboo on tools. Their eyes challenged him to disbelieve them, to find out for himself.

"Other than the feeling of being watched," he said carefully, "have you had any sign, any other evidence or indication of somebody, or something? I know about the feeling, because I feel it too. And very strongly, right now. But any specific evidence?"

Jed Dawkins looked relieved at the confession.

"Everything's the evidence. Everything that's happened. What more evidence would you want?" he said.

"One of the strongest arguments in favor of something, or some kind of intelligence," Cal said slowly, "is that nobody's been hurt. All natural law hasn't been canceled. We still have light radiation, heat radiation, gravity, water still flows, the planet still turns. Trees still grow and fruit still ripens. We can talk and be understood, using our tongues and minds as tools. We can still eat and drink. We can still know.

"This is no chaotic co-ordinate system that defies all natural law. This is a deliberate manipulation of some natural laws to get a result. Man manipulates natural laws by the use of tools and materials, but he doesn't suspend them. Here, apparently without tools, at least tools we can perceive, natural law is manipulated, but not suspended.

"When the village disappeared, no one was hurt. A lot of people were caught in awkward positions and fell, some of them several feet. There should have been at least a few broken bones, pulled ligaments. There weren't. Our ship landed safely. We were a long time in the atmosphere of Eden, and for a few minutes there on the ground we were still using tools of a high order. It was only when danger of real harm to us was past that the ship disappeared."

"I reckon it's comfortin' to know we ain't meant to be hurt," Jed said, and looked at his two companions. "I guess it is," he repeated doubtfully. "Maybe it ain't something as nice and familiar as a cyclone, or a den of rattlesnakes, something you could understand, but you got to admit we ain't been hurt yet." It was as if he were arguing the point with his companions.

"Something I've been noting, Jed," Ahmed spoke up. "A discrepancy of a sort that has me puzzled. Sun reckoning, we've been able to keep our minds on this subject for over two hours now. As if, whatever this is manipulating natural laws can also manipulate the way our minds work."

"Yeah," Jed admitted slowly, his face thoughtful. He turned to Cal. "Like I said at the start. Our minds have sort of wandered of late. Start to do something, and first thing y'know, we're doin' something else. Can't keep our minds on one thing very long—like animals."

"That might be no more than the aftermath of deep shock," Cal said.

"It's for a purpose!"

Startled at the outburst, they all turned and looked at Louie.

"It's for a purpose," Louie repeated in a kind of rapture. "They want us to understand we are being watched over, cared for. That colonist you all laughed at was right. This is the first Garden of Eden, where man lived in complete innocence. Now man has been returned to it, to live again in complete innocence. You do not think straight because there is no reason. You will be cared for. Woe unto him who seeks to despoil it again by seeking vain knowledge!"

His eyes were wild, his face contorted with a mixture of exaltation and condemnation.

"Shut up, Louie," Tom said in a low, firm voice.

"We understand," Jed said tolerantly. "Some of the colonists are talkin' the same way. He's got plenty of company."

18

All the rest of that day, and throughout the following, Cal and Tom worked with Jed in trying to round up the colonists, get them living together again.

By agreement, Ahmed and Dirk stayed with the small band of colonists that had overcome their fears enough to mingle together again. Louie frankly deserted his shipmates, and spent all his time with the colonists. Frank, as if reverting to his childhood farming days, occupied himself with trying to round up the stock. He tried to keep the cows separated from their calves so the colonists would have milk to drink, but without ropes or corrals it was hopeless. He finally gave up his attempt to husband the stock, and he too seemed content then to mingle with the colonists.

The marked change in Louie could not be ignored, for he was not idling away his time in lazy feeding and sleeping. He had dropped his lifelong pose of superficial complaint that the fates always gave him the dirty end of the stick, and now he spent his time preaching to the little band of colonists. Or wandering through the forests and undergrowth calling, praying, comforting.

Cal felt no condemnation for him. He was not the first man, seemingly dedicated to science, who, confronted with mysteries beyond his power to comprehend, reverted to childlike superstitious awe for an explanation. In the face of mystery or catastrophe, it takes a faith beyond the capacity of most to continue believing that the universe has a rational order to its laws that can be comprehended if man persists. It is temptingly easy for man to revert back to the irresponsibility of childhood, assuming that the control of phenomena is in the hands of those stronger, wiser than he. It takes a strength, in the face of this temptation, to go on believing that man *can* know, that it is not morally wrong for him to know.

No blame then for Louie.

Tom was torn in his loyalties. He frequently remembered that away from E.H.Q. the crew become the E's attendants, and that their first duty is always to the E. But separation from the other two men of his crew was like the loss of a part of himself. To these also he had a duty. He tried to solve his problem by alternating his time, spending part of it with Cal, the remainder with his crew.

Cal and Jed made a trip the following morning across the ridge, and found the dissident group huddled together in abject terror. They had seen the ship coming down through the atmosphere and, all together, they had climbed the ridge, where one of their scouts had recently gone, to watch the ship's landing—and its disappearance.

Once they were found, it took little persuasion to convince them they should return to the other colonists, that differences of opinion meant nothing now as against the need of human beings to cling together in the face of catastrophe.

But they too were having trouble thinking in a straight line, and even though they first appeared eager to join the other colonists, it took some doing to keep them all together and moving forward to cross the ridge, to come down the other side, to assemble again at the site of the village with the others.

And yet, within minutes, neither band seemed to remember that they had ever been separated.

By the time they had returned, it was apparent that Louie was succeeding where Jed had failed in finding the colonists. In the few hours that had elapsed, the nucleus had tripled in size. Louie's wandering through the brush, calling, pleading with them to follow him, promising there was no danger if they would allow him to watch over them, intercede for them with Those who had caused all this, had indeed coaxed them from their hiding places, calmed their fears.

And still through the day he toiled, finding them, bringing them back into the fold, one and two and three at a time, until, at last, by Jed's count, all were there, no more missing.

And yet, in spite of his success, there was a kind of hurt and disappointment in Louie's eyes. For once back, they not only forgot their fears, they seemed also to forget him. They coalesced into a placid herd, without memory of their panic. Without memory of the shepherd who had found the lost sheep and returned them to the fold.

They wandered among the trees and bushes, picking fruit and nuts, eating leaves and stems and flowers of plants. They wandered down to the river to lie prone on the sand, dip their faces into the clear cold water to drink. During the heat of the day they bathed in the river, and as they lay on white sand or grassy slopes to dry, they slept contentedly.

The phenomenon was not as startling to Cal as it might have seemed to others.

On Earth, gradually learned through trial and error, experimental colonists were not picked for their jobs because of flexible, incisive, or brilliant minds. Quite the contrary. The basic test of a successful colonist was endurance—the endurance of hardship, privation, the stoic indifference to conditions of discomfort, monotony, pain, uncleanliness, immodesty—conditions which would send a more imaginative or sensitive temperament into a downward-spiraling syndrome of failure. They were the kind of men and women who, on Earth in an earlier time, had been able to endure the harshness of the sea, of arctic cold, jungle disease, desert heat; to make those first steps in taming a hostile environment, so that men with less endurance, but with more delicately poised and sensitive minds, following them might then endure.

It was characteristic of such men and women, even under Earth conditions, that they seldom questioned their reasons for these things. They simply went, and endured, and tamed. Even on Earth, when the taming had been done, they moved on. This was the stuff of the experimental colonist.

Now, here, that temperament still persisted. They had fled in panic, but now they had returned to their original purpose—to endure. It was enough.

Louie was to learn, in disappointment, that failure to be curious about scientific reasoning was usually accompanied by an equal failure to be curious about philosophical implications. They listened idly to his exhortations, but their eyes did not light with fire nor cloud with doubt. They simply wandered away after a time and ate or slept.

In the evening of that second day, Cal sat with Tom and Jed down by the bank of the river where the sky was clear and the stars beginning to shine. They were talking quietly of home, of Eden, of the colonists who, more and more, seemed to take on the character of a contented herd of animals. So far there had been no attempt of the old males to drive the young ones out of the herd, destroy them, but that might come in time; as surely as the old males on Earth by tacit agreement on both sides, were always able to work up a war for the purpose of weeding out and destroying lusty young male competition.

They were talking of the curious fact that all three of them seemed able to continue thinking in a straight line, hold their minds to a subject, while all the rest grew more vague, less retentive, more content to live from moment to moment, without concern for past or future.

Except Louie. He too seemed able to hold his thinking in a straight line, one tangential to theirs. He seemed, in these hours, to have turned wholly mystical, to a stronger belief that they were being watched and cared for by some higher power, and that this was for a purpose. Yet not so tangential, for Cal had come to the same conclusion, although his interpretation differed.

"I can't doubt that there is an intelligent direction of this peculiar co-ordinate system," he said to Tom and Jed. "But I must doubt it is supernatural in the way Louie interprets. Anything appears to be magic when we don't understand how it happens, and becomes science when we do."

He paused, and looked at his companions' faces in the starshine. They were quiet, reposed, listening.

"Ever since man got up off the bottom of his ocean of air," he said, "and out into space, we've been prepared to run into some form of intelligence which doesn't behave the way we do. Not prepared to do anything about it, you understand," he said with a shrug. "Just theoretically prepared that it might happen. It was a possibility. Now it does seem to have happened. E McGinnis asked me, before I left Earth, if I thought Eden was an alluring trap, especially baited to catch some human beings. It begins to appear that it is."

"I've caught many a wild animal in my day," Jed said slowly, thoughtfully. "I've pinned 'em up in cages, watched how they behaved. I guess scientists do that all the time. Don't want to hurt 'em, fact make 'em as comfortable as they can—just want to know about 'em. Sometimes, after I watched them awhile I'd turn 'em aloose and watch 'em scoot back to their natural world. That could happen to us. Sometimes they'd die, and I wouldn't know why. That could happen. Some animals won't bear young in captivity. We can't because of an operation. Maybe whatever's holdin' us don't know that, and might turn us aloose when, after a time, we don't bear any young."

He paused and looked even more thoughtful.

"Sometimes," he added slowly, "after I studied 'em, found out how they would behave no matter what, I had to kill 'em, because they was too dangerous to let run around among humans. That could happen."

"I haven't done much trapping," Tom said. "But in zoos I've

watched animals in cages. The thought always came to me that if they could think the way we do, they could just open their cages and walk away."

"Now you take turkeys," Jed answered. "Pin 'em up with a high fence, they'll back up, take off and fly over it. But pin 'em with a low fence, and they won't. Seems like they know they have to fly over a high obstruction, but don't figger on it for a low one. Sometimes they flutter up against it, or try to push it over, but most of the time they just walk around and around in the yard lookin' for an opening."

"Natural survival pattern," Cal commented. "In the woods, in their natural state, when they came up against a fallen log, it took more effort to lift their heavy bodies in flight over it than it took to walk around the log. It became a fixed pattern of behavior to walk around it."

"That's what they do with a low fence then," Jed said. "They just keep tryin' to walk around the obstruction. Not enough sense to treat it like a high fence, because it ain't high, see? No use tryin' to tell 'em it's high, because they know it ain't. So they can't solve it. Seems awful stupid, somehow, a little low fence, all that blue sky above 'em, and they can't figger it out."

"I suspect that's what's happening to us," Cal said. "We've always argued that wherever there is matter and energy in the universe, certain natural laws will prevail. We've learned ways to take advantage of those natural laws, to do certain things that will make them work for us instead of against us.

"We've always argued that for any kind of intelligence to arise in the universe it, too, would have to become aware of these natural laws; that it, too, would have to do these same certain things to take advantage of those laws; that because the laws and what to do about them would always be similar man would have a lot in common with that other intelligence, and a means of communicating because of that similarity.

"We'd argue that whatever its evolutionary physical shape, this wasn't so important as its mental evolution—because that mental evolution would follow the same course as ours. They wouldn't be truly alien, because science would be a common denominator.

"Now it appears we could be wrong. Maybe our concept of science is too narrow. Maybe we're like the turkey. We've become so fixed in our pattern of solving a problem we can't change, can't back off and take another look, see the problem not as it appears but as it really is."

"But isn't that the science of E?" Tom asked curiously. "To be able to extrapolate any co-ordinate system? I'm not criticizing," he added hastily. "Just asking."

"I suspect even our means of extrapolation are too limited, too based on the relationship of things and forces to each other, too set in the notion that only physical tools can affect physical things. We may be looking at a low fence, calling it a log, and therefore not able to understand why we can't walk around the obstruction in the usual manner." He stopped, and added with a shrug. "Stupid, maybe. Or like the turkey, the yard is so big that he never gets a picture of it as a whole enclosure. By the time he's wandered down this side of the fence he's forgot what he found on the other side. Never can put the whole thing together in his mind. That's my trouble, anyhow. So far, I'm not able to put the whole thing together, see it all as one piece.

"When I do, if I do, then maybe like a caged animal I'll see how to unlock an opening, or maybe realize the only way out is to fly."

There beside the softly flowing river, where water was obeying natural law without any trouble, the three men broke off their discussion when they saw a bright flash high in the sky above them. All three knew what it meant.

Another E ship had arrived.

No doubt the ship would expect light signals from the colonists in acknowledgment of their space flare.

If the ship had come while this portion of the planet was still in daylight, they would have seen there was no village, no ship, no equipment for direct communication. They may even have reasoned there was no means of signaling with artificial light.

But there was nothing to tell them that those on Eden could not build a fire.

As if they were present on the ship themselves, the three men could anticipate what must be happening there. Right now they would be anxiously waiting for signal flares to light up, to spring up like signal fires on a lonely island where a marooned man has, at last, sighted a ship on the horizon.

The colonists were no longer hiding, but were freely wandering in open spaces. If the ship had arrived before dusk they would have seen the men and women in the viewscopes. If after dusk, they still might have spotted them in the infrared viewers which picked up the heat differentials and gave a fair approximation of shapes.

The men on the ship would be waiting and looking at their watches. How long, they would be asking, does it take those colonists, that E down there, to get a signal fire going?

About five minutes passed, and another flare lighted the heavens.

"Get off the dime down there!" it seemed to say. "Acknowledge us!"

Cal took the chance that they might have an infrared viewscope directly on him, and he waved his arms above his head. But apparently they had not spotted him, for there was no answering flare.

At intervals of five minutes at first, then later cut to fifteen minutes, throughout the long night the flares continued to light the sky.

"Talk to us," the flares begged. "Surely you were expecting us. Surely you would not all be sleeping so soundly that our light could not rouse you."

Several times the three men stood up and waved their arms, but it brought no answer from the ship. In the darkness perhaps the equipment wasn't good enough. Perhaps in the night breeze bushes and trees also swayed with movement.

Once there was a rustle in the brush, and in the starlight they recognized the figure of Louie approaching them.

"This has got to stop," he said worriedly as he came up to them. "That light is an unnatural thing. It will anger Them. It is not meant for the peace of Eden to be disturbed by any artificial thing. And if They should turn Their wrath upon us—woe, woe!"

His face was stricken in the light of a new flare, and as suddenly as he had come to object, he left, plunged back under the trees to seek his people, be beside them, comforting them when disaster struck down.

After a time the three men gave up trying to wave their acknowledgment of the flares in darkness. They watched for an hour or so, and then tried to sleep. The periodic flares continued to come throughout the long night, as if now no longer pleading for acknowledgment, but rather reassuring men in such deep distress that they could not answer. Reassuring them that help was at hand and morning would come.

They tried to sleep, and although fitfully disturbed by the continuing flares, they did sleep. But at the first hint of dawn, Cal awoke and aroused his two companions, and by the time there was enough light for the ship to see clear detail upon the ground, the three men were ready for a better attempt at answering the ship's signal.

They went up to the village site, where the colonists were sleeping in the way a herd is bedded down together. They awoke Frank and Martha, Ahmed and Dirk, and told them of their plan. Louie, too, awoke, heard the plan, and tried to warn them against it. Any attempt, he said, to communicate with those not on Eden would surely increase the wrath of Those who wanted only the natural state here—a wrath still withheld because of superhuman mercy, but which must not be tried too far.

In spite of his warnings, Cal, and those co-operating with him, got together enough colonists to carry out his plan.

Good-naturedly, the colonists did as they were told, but with the attitude that it was something amusing, that there was nothing they'd rather be doing at the moment. Any sense of urgency about communicating with home seemed to have been washed from their minds.

In a clear space, on the soft grass, Cal got the colonists to sit or lie in certain positions. Checked against Tom's knowledge of ancient signal patterns, those certain positions took the shape of space-navy patterns.

Three men lay in a triangle. Next to that, six men sat in a circle, and last three more men lay in another triangle. Cal hoped someone on the ship would be able to read the ancient message.

"Keep clear of me. I am maneuvering with difficulty."

The signal had no more than formed when there was a flash from the ship so bright that it could be seen in the morning sky. They had read his signal, and now they began a series of flashes, of questions. "What's going on down there?" was the essence of their questioning.

It was well the ship had caught the first signal, for the colonists lost all interest in the game which had no point. They simply stood up and wandered away in search of their breakfasts from the trees and bushes.

Louie, who had stood to one side glowering, now took charge of them again and shepherded them to a grove of trees where the fruit seemed especially large and succulent.

But now that the ship had spotted him, Cal could signal alone. He lay down on the ground, himself, to move his arms in semaphore positions. But even as he lay back, he became conscious that he, too, could hardly care less. With a detached interest that amounted to amusement at such childish, primitive things, he watched his arms spell out one more message.

"Keep off! No mechanical science allowed in this co-ordinate system."

He stood up then, and made a farewell gesture toward the ship.

At that instant he felt strangely that he had passed into another stage of growth, completed a task, cut himself off from an environment that had held him back. What the ship did, in response to his warnings, no longer mattered. If it landed, its personnel too would join the colonists. If it obeyed the request of an E, it might circle there indefinitely.

Indefinitely watching the turkeys circle inside their low fence, unable to aid them, release them.

He did not particularly care what they did.

They could go on, spluttering out their signals, trying to question him. He didn't even try to read their messages. It didn't matter. Their science had nothing to do with him, nothing to offer him. Through it he could not reach a solution.

Somehow he knew that already.

19

"This time," the communications supervisor said with all the firmness he could muster, "this time there must not be any interference with communication. There just absolutely must not be!"

"Well, it wasn't my fault," the operator retorted with an exasperation that blanketed prudent restraint. "You heard what E McGinnis said—that they could identify E Gray, and the ship's crew, and many of the colonists, but that there was no sign of the ship that took them there. If there wasn't any ship there couldn't be any communication. It's not my fault. I can't receive something that wasn't sent."

"I know, I know," the supervisor said, and then, worried that he may be giving the appearance of backing down, commanded savagely, "just watch it, that's all!" He chewed violently at his knuckle and glared at the operator.

"Just watch it," the operator mumbled bitterly. "Just watch it, the man says. And what will I watch if the message stops coming?"

"Now, now, now, now," the supervisor nagged, "we'll have no insubordination, if you please."

And upstairs this time more than Bill Hayes, sector chief, were monitoring the message. The top administrative brass of E.H.Q. were assembled in their big plush conference room used for arriving at major policy decisions that sometimes affected the whole course of man's progress and direction in occupying the universe.

They sat in worried silence as E McGinnis reported the two messages he had received from Junior E Gray.

First: Keep clear of me. I am maneuvering with difficulty.

Then: Keep off. No mechanical science allowed in this co-ordinate system.

They looked at one another under beetled brows. They wondered, at first privately and then openly if that Junior E had blown his stack. They had looked at many a problem finally solved by the E's, but never before had such a ridiculous situation come up.

And right at the time, too, when the civil government had decided to place a curb on E.H.Q.'s freedom of movement, its control over the experimental phases of planet development. The injunction to halt a Junior E from taking over the Eden problem fooled none of them. They knew that Gunderson wasn't concerned for those colonists out there, that he was merely using the public furor to advance his own personal power. They knew that the police worked unremittingly, unceasingly, always and ever to bring every phase of human activity under their control. They knew it was a centuries-old tactic to wait for the right situation to arise, so that the lawmakers could be stampeded into passing some law which seemed only to apply to this given condition but in actuality broadened police powers over a wide area of man's actions.

Yes, there was far more at stake here than the fate of fifty colonists. In a sense E.H.Q. itself was the stake. The whole science of E was at stake.

And E McGinnis had played right into Gunderson's hands. It was he who had been the E influence in deciding to allow a Junior to handle the problem in the first place. It was he who was standing off from the planet, not landing and taking over things as he should.

There was obviously no danger. By his own report, the people on Eden were in good health, and from their apparent actions, not even distressed.

This message about no mechanical science being allowed, for example. Did the Junior mean the colonists wouldn't allow it? Must mean that. What else could prevent it? But when an E, a real E, took charge in an experimental colony, the colonists had nothing further to say about the matter. True, when the five-year experimental period was over and the three-generation colonists took over a planet, then it came more under civil control, and E.H.Q. largely withdrew with the provision that it could step back in at any time the problem seemed not to have been solved after all.

But while under the five-year test . . . The E was the final word, or should be. The colonists knew it. The E knew it, or should know it. Obviously then it was weakness on the part of the Junior if he allowed the colonists to dictate that there could be no mechanical science. Proof of his inability to handle the job.

A perfect setup for Gunderson!

They decided they were forced to take a strong hand with McGinnis. Ordinarily the E was the final word, not only with the colonists, but with the administration at E.H.Q. But maybe there were times when he shouldn't be. Yes, definitely they should take a hand. After all, Gray was still a Junior, hardly more than a boy. Was it right that a mere boy could stop investigation by anyone except himself? Tell Earth with all its power and might what to do?

Definitely there was a time when an exception to general E policy should be made. Definitely this was that time. If nothing else, they must take a strong hand to prevent Gunderson from moving in with his police powers. Protect the E science from Gunderson, or at least salvage what they might.

Their conference over, they asked for a connection with McGinnis.

"We assume you will land and take charge, E McGinnis?" the board chairman asked.

"Certainly not," McGinnis snapped back. "An E has forbidden it."

"Well now," the chairman argued, and sweat began to come out on his forehead. "He's only a junior. We have decided his judgment isn't mature enough for this problem."

"I have every confidence in Junior E Gray," McGinnis said acidly. "And every E in the system will back me. It makes no difference what you have decided. Either the science of E means something, or it doesn't. Either we have complete freedom to handle a problem, or we don't. Let me remind you, gentlemen, this isn't the first time that laymen have decided the E is a fool and tried to take matters into their own hands. Do you want to repeat past disasters?"

"If we don't land a ship, E McGinnis"—the chairman was all but pleading now—"Gunderson's police will. We feel we must land a ship to take a firmer control over the situation. Public sentiment demands it. Policy demands it. Perhaps the whole future of E demands it."

A new voice cut into the communications hookup, a feminine voice.

"Gentlemen," she said, "this is Linda Gray. I requested that I be cut in on any communication concerning my husband, and E McGinnis made it an order before he left. If another ship does land, I must be on it. I want to be with my husband."

"I will not be landing on Eden, Linda," E McGinnis said firmly. "An E has forbidden it. That is enough for any other E in the universe. No other E will land. Your husband is all right. He is in good health, and apparently mentally sound. At least sound enough to warn us against landing. He must have a reason. We don't know, yet, what it is.

"Now he has stopped communicating, we don't know why. He must have a reason for that, too. It is probably a sound reason. E science has been drilled into him until it is a part of his every mind cell, perhaps even every body cell.

"I assume he is not communicating because we can't help him, because communicating with us distracts him from solving the problem. If E.H.Q. decides to send out a ship on its own, and risk landing in an unknown co-ordinate system, against the orders of two E's, which will become the combined orders of all E's in the universe, that is their decision. If you wish to be on it, that is your decision.

"I am cutting off now. It will be no accident that E.H.Q. cannot connect with me. I'm cutting out because I don't want to be distracted any further. I'm trying to think."

The acid rebuff of the old E left the administrative board hanging in a vacuum of indecision, frustration. Angry determination to do something, anything.

They were caught between the intransigence of the E fraternity it was their duty to serve and from whom they should be able to expect help, and the obvious determination of Gunderson to use this incident as his means of regaining control over the E's and E.H.Q. for civil authority. Didn't the stupid E see the danger? Wasn't it the same danger that men of science had always faced, the same mistake they had always made—leaving out the human element in a problem?

The eternal blind spot in men of science! The average man doesn't give a tinker's damn for progress or knowledge, not really. He wants only that he and his shall be ascendant at the center of things, the inevitable, the only possible goal of the non-science mind. Surely the history of science versus non-science should have made this evident long ago! Surely there had been enough incidents in history. . . .

Very well, it was up to them to help the E in spite of himself. If he refused the see the clear danger to his whole structure— and their own ascendant position at the center of it—it was their clear duty to protect him nonetheless.

They would send out another ship, a large one, a floating laboratory, a miniature E.H.Q., at least to be there on the scene; to help in any way they could, perhaps to counter the moves Gunderson's police might make, at least to stand by.

At least, in the face of all this public clamor about Eden, to show their concern. The chairman of the board rationalized it masterfully, without once mentioning that their real concern was to remain ascendant at the center of things at all costs, and thereby maintained the tradition of all non-science endeavors.

"Gentlemen," he said in summary, "we have a grave responsibility not only to the E structure, but to all mankind as well. In every system, in every rule, there must be provision for the exception. Gray is only a Junior E. Herein lies the weakness of our position. Herein lies Gunderson's strength, his weapon for swaying the sentiment of the people. A Junior E is not mature enough to make the decisions affecting the life or death of fifty people. More than that, perhaps the future progress of mankind.

"May I point out, gentlemen, that in a showdown, if it should become necessary for us to land a ship to rescue those colonists, in spite of the Junior's demand that we stay clear of the planet, we will not be overriding the decision of an E, but of a boy who has not yet proved his capacity to merit an E.

"We have to draw the line somewhere. I am forced to agree with Gunderson on that. If we must honor the command of the Junior E, then why not the Associate E? Why not the student E? Why not the apprentice student E? Why not any kid in the universe who thinks he is extra smart?

"The line of demarcation, the point at which civil control over the individual gives way to immunity from civil control has never been clearly drawn. We may regret that the issue has arisen at all, but it has arisen. Gunderson's purpose is clear. He intends to bring the E structure back under civil control. We must salvage what we can. Perhaps if we concede his control over the Juniors on down, we can maintain the immunity of the Senior E. We must work to save at least that much."

The floating laboratory, which might have to become a rescue ship, left six hours later.

Linda was on it.

20

There was no frustration, no uncertainty in Gunderson's mind.

His course was now clear. His observer ship had also read the messages spelled out by the placement of naked bodies on the grass, and in the semaphore wavings of the Junior E's arms. The photographs taken were all the evidence he needed to prove the morals charges he intended to bring.

It might not be wise to allow the total photographs to show in the newspapers, on television, for there were ex-navy men here and there who might interpret the code. But enlarged pictures of the individuals, separated from the total, disporting themselves in lewd, naked positions would do the job.

Clearly the police must put a stop to this. He would have every organization in the universe dedicated to dictating the morals of others on his side. No politician would have the guts to stand up in opposition.

There remained only one thing to do. Go out and get that Junior E, place him under arrest, bring him back for trial. Perhaps it might be wise to let the colonists off easy—he could easily show that it was the influence of the Junior which had made a disgusting orgy develop there on Eden. Never mind that they were naked before the Junior arrived. The public could always be razzle-dazzled about the nature of the evidence, its order and meaning. It was an old police, prosecution, and political trick to separate a few items from the total context, but still a good one; for the public never bothered to know the whole context of anything. An old trick to fasten on phrases and slogans to fix an attitude in the public mind, for a phrase or slogan was about all the public was able to master. Anyone who had ever served on a jury, observed its deliberations, knew that out of all the welter of evidence, only certain isolated statements or facts, often minor and insignificant, penetrated the juror's mind, and around these bits he formed his conclusions. Any smart lawyer knew that, and tried to set up his case accordingly.

His own course was clear.

His orders to the selected captain of his police ship were equally clear:

1. *Proceed at once to Eden, the scene of the crime.*
2. *Ignore any protests from the E ship already out there, or any other ship E.H.Q. might have sent.*
3. *Ignore any signals from the Junior E on the planet.*
4. *Land on the planet at the site of Appletree, the main site of the lewd and obscene crime.*
5. *Place Junior E Calvin Gray under arrest.*
6. *Place the crew of the Junior E's ship, Thomas Lynwood, Franklin Norton, Louis LeBeau, under arrest.*
7. *Place any colonist who opposed the police under arrest.*
8. *Place the remainder of the colonists in detention under protective custody.*
9. *Place E McGinnis under arrest if he interfered in any way with the police in carrying out the foregoing orders.*

The police captain raised his eyebrows when he read the final order.

Place a Senior E under arrest?

Certainly, a Senior E. It was one thing to allow these birds to wander around, free as air to do as they please. It was one thing to let them get away with making such statements as "The police attitude toward the people is the major cause of crime." It was something else, and time the E's found it out, for them to make any overt move to interfere with the police in their performance of duty.

Personally, he hoped the old E would be fool enough to resist. It would strengthen his case.

The police captain obeyed the first of the orders without a hitch. He proceeded to the scene of the crime.

He obeyed the second order. He ignored the command of E McGinnis, received over the ship's communicator when they arrived at the scene of the crime, to stand clear of the planet. What policeman moving in to make an arrest for an illegal act— and certainly running around stark naked, posing in lewd and indecent postures in full view of the public, was an illegal act— would pay any attention to the request of an onlooker which amounted to "Aw, let 'em alone, copper"?

There was no communication at all from the Junior E on the planet's surface, so the third order did not apply.

It was in trying to execute the fourth order that he ran into trouble.

He passed inside the orbits of the three other ships now circling the planet, the police observer ship, the E McGinnis ship, the E.H.Q. floating laboratory. He gave orders to lower his ship into Eden's atmosphere.

The proper buttons were pushed, the proper levers pulled.

And nothing happened.

It was as if some invisible shield held him back. He could not lower the ship into the atmosphere gently, taking the normal precautions against crashing. Very well then, not so gently. Full power. And nothing happened. They lowered not another inch.

A thrust. A thrust at tangent to the surface. Once past whatever this barrier was, they could skim the surface and come back to land on the proper site. They backed the ship farther out into space. They made their thrust with full speed and momentum.

There was no sensation when they hit the barrier, but they did not penetrate it. It was as if a flat stone had been skipped across slick ice, and they shot back out into space again. The tangent penetration would not do.

Very well, then. A direct thrust, full power, straight down. Be prepared to put braking forces into immediate power, lest they crash the ship at full power against the surface.

And again, no sensation. Against all natural laws of inertia, they came to a full stop at the given level outside the atmosphere without any feeling of jar or opposing pressure at all.

What now, Mr. Gunderson, sir?

Reluctantly, Gunderson ordered the police captain to contact E McGinnis. E science apparently had some kind of shield which they'd kept secret from the people—and wouldn't there be a stink over that one, once he released that information! Contact E McGinnis and find out!

"Why sure," E McGinnis cackled with derisive laughter, "sure there's a shield. I didn't make it. I wouldn't know how. No, I don't know what's causing it. But I'll tell you what I think. I think They've caught the specimen They want. There's an E down there.

"So, naturally, the trap door is closed."

21

Cal didn't know, couldn't have known, that his efforts to signal McGinnis not to land were unnecessary. Didn't know, couldn't have known, that he himself was the specimen They had hoped to catch. That having caught what They wanted They would naturally close the door to the trap to prevent any possibility of escape, as yet, or any interference with their experiment.

From the moment he walked away from the grassy slope where he had signaled the outer ship, he moved and thought as someone detached from ordinary existence. As he walked away from the slope, ignoring the frantic signals from the ship out in space, he felt he was also walking out of a shell of superficial cerebration and into a deeper sense of reality. It was as if, in spite of E training, for the first time in his life, he could commit himself wholly, in all areas of his being, to the consideration of a problem.

His conviction was complete that the ship could give him nothing he needed, that all Earth's mechanical science could give him nothing he needed. That it could not provide the key to unlock the door which led into this new area of reality. He must find, must define, some new concept of man's relation to the universe. He must again travel that road, that million-year-long road man had traveled in trying to determine his position in reality.

He wandered down to the river, climbed to the top of a great boulder that overhung a pool, and sat down with his feet hanging over the edge. He watched some young colonists wade through the pool to drive fish into the shallows where they could pin them, with their legs, catch them with their hands. In their need for protein, the colonists were finding, as many Earth peoples had found, raw fish were excellent in flavor and texture as food.

At the beginning of the road man had traveled first there was awareness, awareness of self as something separate from environment. There was awareness of self-strength, ability to do certain things to and with that environment. There was awareness of self always at the center of things, and therefore awareness of his importance in the scheme of things. But there was awareness of more.

There was awareness of things happening to his environment which he, in all his strength and importance, could not do. Awareness gives rise to reason, reason gives rise to rationalization. If things happened in his environment which he himself could not do, then there must be something stronger and more important than he.

To be ascendant at the center of things, to remain ascendant, meant that all things of lesser importance, outside the center, must be made subservient to him, else that ascendancy was lost. And if they would not assume positions of subservience, they must be destroyed.

If there were unseen beings, stronger and more important than he, who could do unexplained things to his environment; then it was plain that he must assume positions of subservience to those beings, lest he himself be destroyed.

So man created his gods in his own image, with his own attributes magnified.

Was this a wrong turning of the road? No-o . . . Awareness carries with it its commands and penalties. A problem must have an answer. Conscious and willful beings beyond his own strength and importance became the only answer open to him at that stage of his mental evolution. And served the important need of bringing order to chaos. Let all things he could not do, and therefore could not understand, be attributed to those higher beings. Without such an answer, awareness without resolution would have driven him into madness. Without such an answer, man could not have survived to remain aware.

But answers also carry in themselves their commands and their penalties. The penalty being that when one thinks he has the answer he stops looking for it. The command being that he must conduct himself in accord with the answer.

The long, long road that led him nowhere. That today still leads untold millions nowhere. For the penalty of a wrong answer is failure to solve the problem. That non-science had failed to provide any answer beyond the primitive one was self-evident.

To some, then, it became evident that the question must be reopened. Through the long written history of man, here and there, by accident often, sometimes by cerebration, the use of the brain with which he was endowed, man found on occasion he could do things to his environment that heretofore had been the province of the gods—and in the doing had not become a god! To the courageous, the brave, the daring, the foolhardy questions then that demanded new answers.

Perhaps the most daring and courageous question of all time was asked by Copernicus: What if man is not at the center of the universe, the reason for its creation?

He personally escaped the penalties for asking it. The question was too new, too revolutionary for the men of his day to grasp, for the non-science leaders, secure in their ascendancy at the center of things, to see in it the threat to their ascendancy. It was on his followers, those who saw sense in the question, that the wrath of non-science descended. Non-science used the only method it had ever devised to achieve the only result it had ever been able to countenance—torture and force to make dissidents kneel in subservience.

But the question had been asked! And once asked, it could not be erased!

Still, it was almost an accidental question. For the method of science, as something understood and communicable, as a calculated point of view, had not yet been discovered. The key that would unlock its door had not yet been found.

Cal lay back on the rock to bathe in the warm rays of Ceti, almost to doze, yet with thought running clear and unimpeded. The splashing and the laughter of the colonists below the rock were no more than accompanying music.

The key which opened the door to physical science was not discovered until 1646 by a bunch of loafers, ne'er-do-wells, beatniks, who hung around the coffee shops of London. Later, because non-science always persecutes those who dare ask questions and thereby demonstrate some subversion to subservience, many had to flee to Oxford which, at that time, was sanctuary for those who differed from popular thought.

As he lay there drinking in the sun, the peacefulness, he sent his vision back through the card index of his mind to find the reference, the key that opened the door to physical science, the pregnant point of view that would give birth to a whole new concept of man's relationship to the universe. He found the passages in Thomas Sprat's *History of the Royal Society of London* (1667).

". . . to make faithful records of all the works of nature, or art which can come within their reach . . . They have stud'd to make it, not only an enterprise of one season, or of some lucky opportunity; but a business of time; a steddy, a lasting, a popular, an uninterrupted work."

He stirred restlessly and changed his position to lay his head on one arm. Not quite, not yet the key. Ah, here it was, perhaps the most significant sentence ever written by man.

"They have attempted to free it from the artifice, and humors, and passions of sects; to render it an instrument whereby mankind may obtain a dominion over *Things*, and not only over one another's judgements."

That was it. That was the essence of its difference from non-science, for the only method ever discovered until then was the non-science method of making its judgments prevail over all others.

Once this answer was discovered, it too could not be erased in spite of all the efforts of non-science. With that answer, man had come this far.

And now?

Could it be that science, as with non-science, was only a partial answer? Only another stage? Only a section of the road man must travel? Something as limited in its way as non-science was limited? Something too narrow to contain the whole of reality? Something also to be left behind? A milestone passed, instead of the goal?

What comes after science? What new door must be opened into a still newer point of view? What pregnant new concept of his relationship to reality must man now discover before he could continue his journey down the long road toward total comprehension?

He could ask the question, but it was not the right question; for it contained no hint of an answer. He felt an irritation in himself, almost as if some teacher in the past had shaken his head in disapproval.

For a moment he welcomed the distracting shout from one of the colonists, and sat up. In the shallows of the river one of the men had caught a foot long fish and was holding it up in his hands. Delightedly, the others acknowledged his victory, and renewed their efforts. He lay back down again, and stretched his cramped muscles.

Too fast! He had come down the long, long road too fast. He had missed something, something early. Something man had known in pre-science, and had forgotten in science.

These colonists. Would they grow in awareness? Now they seemed only to be a part of their environment, without curiosity, their fears of even the day before forgotten. Wiped away, as though it had never been, was their memory of a previous existence to this. They were wholly at one with their environment—unaware.

Were they to begin the long road? To telescope its distance? Would they be able to continue living without peopling the trees, the streams, the clouds, the winds, with spirits benign and vengeful—created in their own image? Could they continue to live alone in the universe?

Yes, that was the thing he had missed. Loneliness.

In separating himself from the animals, man had cut off his kinship with them. And so he found companionship with the gods. And cutting himself off from the gods. . . .

Loneliness.

Was man the only thing aware throughout the universe? What purpose then his exploration of it? What might he find that he had not already found?

Already, like a minor thread almost unheard in the symphony of exploding exploration, the questions of the artists were already finding themselves woven into music, painting, literature.

"Are we alone? In all this glittering, sterile universe, are there none other than we who are aware?"

The theme would expand as the purposelessness of colonizing still more and more worlds became wider known. The minor would become major, the recessive dominant. The endless aim of non-science to make all others subservient had lost its purpose for those who could still think. The dominion over things instead of people, the goal of science—was that also to lose its purpose for those who could still think? Until man, defeated by purposelessness, sank back in apathy, lost the very willingness to live—and so died?

What if some other awareness did inhabit the universe, sentient —and lonely? What if, farther along in its explorations, it was feeling that apathy? Facing that dissolution?

When one is lonely, the sensible thing is to seek companionship! To discover in companionship purpose not apparent to the alone—or at least hope to discover it.

For companionship there must be communication. And yet the exasperation, the futility of trying to communicate with a friend who always interpreted everything one said and did as meaning something entirely different from the intent.

Some other friend was the normal answer. But what if there were no other? Wouldn't one extra effort, a final attempt to break through that closed mind be made?

All right.

Communication, then. That was wanted. He would try. But if Their frameworks were so different from his that They misinterpreted all his efforts?

He was interrupted by the soft pad of footsteps, bare feet on grass that sprang up to leave no sign it had been trod upon. A young colonist and his wife, hand in hand, laughing gaily, were coming toward him. The man was carrying a fresh-caught fish. They came to a stop at the base of his rock and looked up at him, the Ceti light glinting on their smiling faces.

"We gave Louie a fish because he said it was our duty," the young man said. "I don't remember why it is our duty. Perhaps it is our duty to give you one too."

At least they were being impartial.

22

When he had pulled the scaled skin of the fish away from the flesh, the flesh away from the bones, and eaten his fill, Cal lay back on the rock again, to doze, to continue his search for a means of communicating.

He was now sharply aware of Their presence, of Their urgency, of Their long patience. Awareness! Once man had got over his greedy delight in occupying more and more of the universe simply because he could, to protect himself against the cosmic loneliness that must follow, he too would be searching for awareness.

But he would define it in his own terms, and pass it by if it did not meet those terms.

That there was some other intelligence which had found man instead, Cal did not doubt. The experiment of Eden, the manipulation of natural laws, the denial of physical tools—for what purpose? To clear away the debris which prevented communication of awareness as They defined it?

There was a trace, a minor trace of awareness in man not dependent upon the tools and artifacts of physical science—extrasensory perception, psi. Underdeveloped, because with physical tools its development had been made unnecessary? Because having found the answers with physical tools, man stopped looking for answers other than these?

Was there, then, a science of controlling things, forces, without the use of physical tools? Was there a road of transition from the crude manipulation of things and forces through tools to a manipulation without them? There was precedent in man's science. The elaborate wirings of the first bulky and crude electronic sets, that gave way to a printed diagram of such wirings on a card to obtain the same result?

A step farther? The visual picture, the mental image of the diagram to obtain the same result? But how?

To one whose total orientation is through the use of physical tools (for the material printed on the card diagram was the physical carrier of the current) how to cause the current to follow the mental image of that diagram? With voice and music bathing one's senses simply because one thought of the diagram of a receiver? How?

He felt like the turkey come up against the obstruction of a fence too low to justify the effort of flying over it. Instead of flying, he was walking around and around, looking for an opening, walking in an endless circle.

Circle?

Excitedly, he climbed down from the rock and headed for a patch of bare sand at the river's edge.

In every framework of thought which man had ever devised, the circle was prominent, vital. It played its part in every creed of every race, of every time. It was as essential to the ancient arts of magic as to the current methods of science. It played its part in the movement of planets, the shape of stars, perhaps the essence of the total universe.

Man might be too didactic in requiring that awareness develop a physical science comparable to his own, but surely awareness, whatever form it took, would know the circle.

He sank down on his haunches beside the smooth sand, and with the tip of his finger he quickly drew a circle.

The furrow, scratched in the sand, did not close or smooth out!

He sat back and waited. Nothing happened. It was almost as

if the invisible intelligence were saying, "All right. You are aware of a circle. That was obvious to us from your artifacts. What else do you know?"

He leaned forward, and as nearly as he could estimate, he dotted the center of the circle with a finger, then scratched a radius to the perimeter. It stayed. To one side he drew another line, approximating the radius and in parenthesis he drew a small 2. Beside this he wrote R^2. He drew an equals sign. He scratched the pi sign.

Then he drew another circle and with the palm of his hand he smoothed all its interior. That should be plain enough. The symbols stayed. They understood his mathematics, then. The equation seemed undisturbed, yet there was something wrong with it. He had to look closely at the sand before he saw what it was.

The $=$ had changed to $:$!

Why had they changed the meaning by substituting "proportionate to" for "equals"? He felt a flash of exasperation. Well sure, without tools he could not draw a perfect circle, nor two of them entirely equal. It was pedantic of them to split hairs over that? He must practice, without tools, to draw a perfect circle?

Or was that running around inside his low fence?

He looked down at the sand, and saw the entire scratching was now smoothed out. Apparently he was on the wrong track. Hadn't got what they meant.

He wrote again in the sand: "pi $= 3.14159265. \ldots$"

Again $=$ changed to $:$.

Again he felt his flash of exasperation. It must be obvious by his string of dots that he knew pi had never been exactly resolved. They were being too pedantic. He must exactly resolve it? Yet the numbers could be continued to infinity and never exactly resolved. He looked down again, and the equation was gone.

Wrong track again.

He sat forward, hugged his knees, and stared into the water. The equation had never been exactly resolved, yet man used

it as a constant, an absolute. An obvious fallacy. Was the difference between physical science and psi science based in this
insignificant difference in exactness? Try something else. See
what happens. There was an equation which had proved its effec-
tiveness, upon which the whole science of atomics was based.

"$E = MC^2$," he wrote.

Again $=$ changed to $:$.

What were they saying? That the fallacy lay in using the equals
sign? That the science of psi was one of proportion. But equals
was one of the possible proportions. Had we become walled in
our low fence because we were too dependent upon the exact
balance? Been satisfied to find that answer, and therefore stopped
looking for the possibilities inherent in unbalanced equations?

He looked down at the symbols again half expecting to see
them erased. But they were still there. So he was starting on the
right track. But wait.

Before his eyes he saw the C^2 smooth out, disappear. Only
"$E : M$" remained. Were they saying that dependence upon
constants was the low fence? That man must learn to do without
his firm absolutes? That was the ultimate in relativity: Energy is
proportionate to matter. But so all-inclusive as to be too vague
for use.

For more than three centuries now, controversy had raged over
Einstein's use of C^2 in his expression. Some held that it was a
product of his time, that he was able to make only one step beyond
classical physics where all things must be related to a fixed value.
Others held that its inclusion was a deliberate fallacy; that
Einstein, by his other work, had shown he knew it was a fallacy;
that, tongue in cheek, he inserted it into his equation in full
knowledge that his fellow scientists of his day could not even bear
to think of the awesome concept of things without orientation
to an absolute; that he knew they would reject him entirely, refuse even to consider his thought unless he catered that much to
their superstitions.

The need of the absolute was not mathematical or scientific, but emotional. Man was still tortured by his determination to be the center of things, himself the fixed absolute! The need of a familiar, fixed cave where he might run and hide, close himself in securely when the chaos of storm outside became too frightening to bear. The need of a fixed absolute, whether in philosophy or science, a fixed spot that would not shift.

The science of psi, then, was based in a willingness to shift?

He looked down at the equation, to see if he were still on the track.

It had changed again. Now it read "EδM": The form of the function of energy to matter is variable.

Quickly, another change. "Df (em)": The form of the function and the independent variable of the function vary together.

Still another: "E $=$ f(M)": There is a general relationship of energy to matter.

And then: "F (e,m) $=$ O": There is a general unspecified relationship between energy and matter.

He slapped his hand down on the sand in frustration.

"All right," he said. "You've made your point. And it means about as much as if I said to the turkey, 'All you have to do is fly'."

There was a stir behind him. He turned his head and saw Louie. A deep sigh, almost a sob came from Louie as he stared down at the symbols in the sand.

"They talked to *you*," Louie said brokenly. "I wanted only to serve Them, but it was to *you* They talked."

And all the tragedy of his life was contained therein.

Cal sprang to his feet, and put his arms around the other man's shoulders. The two of them, the bitter and the sympathetic, looked down at the sand. The symbols were still changing, and now read "There is an infinity of relationships between matter and energy, an infinity of forms to be taken by matter as you control the energy."

The signs were wiped out, and the sense of Their presence was gone. Cal felt the withdrawal, the sense of a lesson being over.

He did not regret it, he had enough to think about. But first, there was Louie, racked with broken sobbing.

Here was a man whose life had been a search for certainties, absolutes that would not shift under the weight of his questioning. No doubt in his youth he had turned to the religions of the day —and found them a tissue of rationalizations without contact in reality. Then to science—and found it, too, constantly shifting in its interpretations, making new evaluations as evidence discounted the old. The shock of landing on Eden to drive him back into childhood interpretations again—at last, the clear evidence that had been denied his belief in youth.

Wholehearted in his belief of Them, yet it was not to him They had talked.

"Louie," Cal said slowly. "If you were lonely, very lonely, if you had searched through the years for companionship, and thought you might have found it, would it please you to have that companion drop to his knees, grovel before you? Would this be your idea of companionship?

"What manner of monstrous egotism would require that? What but the incredible vanity of primitive man, to whom life meant nothing more than conquering or being conquered, could imagine such conduct would be pleasing to another intelligence?

"We are men, Louie. If, in our loneliness, we found another intelligence, wouldn't we want an equal exchange instead of abasement? The use of that intelligence to know, to understand, instead of a denial of it?"

Louie twisted out of Cal's embracing arm, and ran stumbling toward the depths of the forest.

23

For another week, perhaps ten days or more, since time measurement had lost its meaning, Cal lived among the colonists, watched their complete retrogression into a state of unawareness. Even the speech which they had retained seemed now to thin and falter as the simplifying of their idea-content no longer required its use.

Only Tom and Jed seemed to retain their orientation to the past, the clarity of awareness. These two spent much time together, seemed always available when Cal needed them, yet did not intrude upon his thought. Frank now seemed one with the colonists. Louie lived on the outskirts of the herd, near the colonists but not of them. He had ceased to exhort, warn, command, argue. His face was closed, told nothing of what he was thinking.

And he had ceased to demand his tithe as intercessor. He was gathering his own food, catching his own fish.

And he seldom let Cal out of his sight.

Tom and Jed helped as best they could by maintaining contact with the old reality. They spent much of the daytime with the colonists. At night they turned their faces to the dark sky to watch the ships, now grown to four, bathed in the light of Ceti like a constellation of bright stars above them. They read the intermittent flashes of light from McGinnis, and from the E.H.Q. laboratory. McGinnis told of the police ship's attempts to break through the barrier surrounding Eden, and its failure. The laboratory told of Linda's presence on board, and now and then flashed out a message to Cal from Linda of her love, her nearness, her faith in hi.n, her desire to be with him, her patience in waiting.

McGinnis told of the arrival of a fifth ship, carrying Gunderson in person. He had been unable to believe his police captain. Unable to believe that the ship could not land at will. He had come in person to take charge, and apparently fumed his frustration in idleness, unable to do anything with the situation, unwilling to go back to Earth and leave it alone.

Tom and Jed told Cal the content of these messages, but to Cal the reports of the police activity seemed noises heard from far away and unrelated to himself. The messages from Linda seemed the haunting strains of a song remembered from long ago.

For his mind was wholly enrapt with the problem. He had been given the key—reality is a matter of proportion, change the concept of proportion and you change the material form—but he had not found the lock and the door it would open. He knew it, but he couldn't do it.

Perhaps Tom might help? Tom was well-grounded in math, had to be for his job as pilot.

"Look, Tom," Cal said one morning after they had given him the night's messages from the ships. He squatted on the ground and brushed away some leaves from an area of dirt. "Watch the equals sign." He scratched a formula in the dirt:

$$\text{``}2 + 2 = 4\text{''}$$

The $=$ changed to $:$. Then to δ . Then through the series of variable relationships.

Tom leaped to his feet from the log where he had been sitting.

"That's crazy," he exclaimed. "It isn't just proportionate, it isn't variable. It equals."

Jed was looking from one to the other, obviously at a loss.

"Well," Cal said drily, "I'm much more interested in what

151

They have to say than in trying to convince Them that They're wrong."

"But if everything were only proportionate and variable," Tom argued, "then you'd have nothing fixed, constant. Why the proportionate relationship might be dependent solely upon choice. Nothing would be solid, dependable."

"Not even the footprints under your feet," Cal answered softly. "Not a house, nor a field of grain, nor a spaceship. Simply alter the choice of proportion—and they aren't there anymore."

24

Throw a key at the feet of a turkey and it is useless to him. Show him the lock it fits, and it is still useless without the knowledge of how to insert the key and turn it. Unlock it for him, and still it is useless without the knowledge of how to push or pull the door.

This was the essence of why so few mastered the simple steps of physical science, the essence of why so few were able to get beyond step two of E science. Anyone could disagree with a statement, but in answer to "What if it not be true, how then to account for the phenomena?" most bogged down at that point, unable to demonstrate with evidence the validity of some other answer.

Everyone knew the equation $E = MC^2$, but few could implement it to build an atomic power plant.

Perhaps the reactions of Tom, that taking away the concept of a balanced equation destroyed all certainty, and therefore was not to be countenanced, was a reflection of his own reaction, willing though he might be to consider something else.

In his wanderings about the island, picking fruits and nuts, stems and leaves, catching fish when he hungered, drinking the clear water of the stream when he thirsted, yet so enrapt that he was unaware he was taking care of his body's needs, Cal built up whole structures of alien philosophies on the nature of the universe, and saw them topple of their own weight.

Until, at last, he realized the basic flaw in all his reasoning. He was too well-grounded in the essence of physical science, and all physical science was built on the balanced equation. Even in trying to consider the unbalanced equation, he had been attempting to determine the exact nature of the unbalance, and to supply it as an X factor on the other side of the equation to restore balance.

To restore balance was to maintain the status quo of physical reality. To turn the key in the lock, to open the door, he must change the physical reality to balance the equation, rather than supply the X factor to keep reality unchanged.

But how to do it still eluded him.

At times, as if seeing partial diagrams, he seemed very close to a solution. At times it seemed the printed card of an electronic wiring was necessary only because the human mind could not visualize the whole without that aid, that music did not come through because in incomplete visualization some little part was left dangling, unconnected. And the long history of non-science belief in the magic properties of cabalistic signs and designs rose up to taunt him, to goad him with the possibility that perhaps man had once come close to the answer of how to control physical properties without the use of tools; that the development of a physical science had taken man down a sidetrack instead of farther along the direct route toward his goal.

Or that man had once been shown, and never understood, or forgot. Yet kept alive the memory that physical shifts could be changed if he could only draw the right design.

Through his wanderings, one fact gradually intruded upon his mind. It seemed the farther inland he roamed, the closer he came to grasping the problem; the nearer the seashore, the more it eluded him.

One morning he looked up at the glittering heights of Crystal Palace Mountain, and suddenly he resolved to climb it. Perhaps the winds of the mountain being stronger, the fuzziness of his thought would be blown away? Perhaps the arrangement of the crystalline structures, the arches and spires, might catch his brain waves, modulate them, transform them, strengthen them, feed them back, himself a part of the design instead of outside it?

In the framework of physical science a nonsense notion. But what harm to try?

He sought out Tom and Jed, the two who would miss him, the two who would care.

"There ain't no water up there, far as I know," Jed said. "And you can't carry none, now. Me and a party scouted the mountain once. It's mighty purty, but useless. The quartz ain't valuable enough to cover its shipping costs back to Earth. The ground is too rocky to farm. Not much in the way of food growing there. So we never went back."

"The scientists surveyed it when the planet was first discovered," Cal said. "One of the first places they went because it was so outstanding. But they found nothing interesting and useful either. Still, I think I'll go."

"Well," Jed said with a shrug. "You can't get lost. If you should lose your bearings, just walk downhill and you'll come to food and water. Follow the shore line until you get back, either direction. And, I reckon, the way things go now, you ain't goin' to hurt yourself. We won't worry about you none. We're all gettin' along all right, so you needn't worry about us either."

"You want me to come with you, Cal?" Tom asked.

"No," Cal answered, "I think better if I'm alone."

He left them then, went past some colonists who were picking berries and eating them, and on up the valley that ran between two ridges.

It was only a few miles to the foothills, a gradual rise of the valley floor, a gradual shallowing and narrowing of the stream, a gradual drawing in of the spokelike ridges until the valley at last became a ravine. The morning air was clear and still, the scent of flowers and ripening fruit was sweet.

Before he left the ravine to begin his climb he ate some of the fruit, and washed the lingering sweet taste from his mouth with a long, cool drink of water from one of the many springs that fed the stream.

He looked up at the mountain above him, and his eye picked out the most likely approach to its summit. It was not a high mountain, not in terms of those tremendous, tortured skin folds of other planets. Hardly more than a high hill in terms of those. Nor, as far as he could see, would the climb be difficult or hazardous.

The fanciful thought of Mount Olympus on Earth came into his mind, although this one was not so inaccessible, so parched and barren. The gods of Greece would have found this a pleasanter place, although they might not have lived so long in the minds of man, since the mountain was more easily climbed, and therefore man would have been the more easily convinced after repeated explorations that no gods lived there after all.

Would the Greeks, as with the later religions, have placed the site of heaven farther and farther away, retreating reluctantly, as man explored the earlier site and found no heaven there? Retreat after retreat until at last the whole idea was patently ridiculous?

Dead are the gods, forever dead, and yet—to what may man now turn in rapture? In ecstasy? In communion? What, in all physical science, filled the deep human need of these expressions?

The climb of the first slope, up to the crest of the ridge he intended to follow, was quickly done. He turned there and looked behind him, at the valley of the colonists below, and far down where the valley merged into the sea, and far on out at the hazy purple line of another island. As he started to turn back again, to resume his climb, his eye caught a flash of something moving in the ravine below him, sunlight on brown, bare skin.

He waited until he caught another glimpse through the trees. As he had suspected it was Louie, still trying to keep him always in sight.

His first impulse was to call out, to wait for Louie, ask him to join in the climb. He discarded the impulse. His need was to get away from all others. And sympathetic and compassionate though he might be, the confusion in Louie's mind seemed to intrude upon his own. Nor had his earlier attempts to comfort Louie met success.

Let Louie follow if he willed. Perhaps the clean air would clear his mind as well. He feared no physical harm, even if Louie's tortured mind intended it. There were no tools to strike at him from a distance. Even a boulder pushed from a height above him would not strike, for that would be the physical use of a tool to gain an end. He feared no bodily attack from ambush, for his own strength and knowledge were dependable.

He began his climb again, followed the crest of the ridge where it swept upward to buttress the side of the mountain. The going was not difficult. The trees and shrubs grew thinner here, and provided clear spaces for him to wind among them. The stones, at first a problem to his bare feet, bothered him less and less until he forgot them. He felt no physical discomfort, neither from tiredness nor thirst, nor from the branches scraping his bare skin, nor anything to drag his mind into trivialities.

Nor tortured theories such as had plagued him in trying to reason out the new concepts of a proportionate, variable reality.

Instead, there was a sense of well being, anticipated completeness, a merging of the often quite separated areas of thought, intuition, and appreciation.

Although at no great height, now the trees no longer grew so tall that they obscured his vision of the heights above. As he climbed they were replaced by shrubs shoulder high, then waist high, then merely low, creeping growths which his feet avoided without mental direction.

A curve of the ridge brought him to the first outcroppings of crystallized quartz. On them he saw no signs of scar left by the geologist's hammer, no imperfections where nodes may have been broken away. They were complete, singularly unweathered.

There was no path, nor hint of one, nor sign that either scientist or colonist had ever passed this way.

The ridge swung back into line, and still he climbed, effortlessly and without consciousness of passing time. Time and space and matter seemed to have receded far into the background of consciousness. Man's star-strewn civilization was no more than a dream. It was as if he, alone and complete, occupied the whole of the universe, encompassed it as he was encompassed by it.

Yet not alone! Their presence, which seemed so evanescent on the valley floor, was closer now, more clearly sensed. Almost as if, at any instant, the veil of blindness would disperse and They would stand revealed.

Now up the final slope of the mountain he threaded his way through higher outcroppings of a more perfectly formed quartz, with deeper amethystine hue scintillating in the Ceti sun's light, diffracted not only in the purples but into greens and reds and blues.

As he came around the base of one of these, there towering above he caught his first full view of the greater spires, pinnacles, buttresses, and arches of the mountain's crest.

It was the crystal palace.

The climb had been steep, steeper than it had appeared from below, yet his breathing was not labored, his mouth was not dry from thirst, nor were his muscles protesting the effort. He did not need to stop and rest, to gather his energy for the last steep assault upon the peak.

Far below him he saw Louie toiling up a slope, then dropping with every appearance of exhaustion when he came to each level place. Still he would rest no more than a minute, and always his head was turned to keep sight of Cal above him. He would push himself to his knees, then to his feet; and slowly, step by step, begin his climb again.

As if from far away, Cal felt a pity at the uselessness of the self-torture, the senseless need of man to punish himself for the guilt of imagined wrongs; and felt a wonder if the strangely developed moral sense of man had not, after all, done more harm than good. For in the ordered universe, where everything fitted into the whole, what could be either good or bad, right or wrong, except as a reflection of man's inadequacies in his imaginings? Rightness and good, wrongness and evil, these could not possibly be other than assessments of furtherance or threat to the ascendancy of me-and-mine at the center of things, and had no meaning beyond that context.

He turned from watching Louie, pitying him, and made the last sharp climb with no more effort than the whole had been. Now he drew near to the towering structures of the crest, now he was beside them. Now he walked beneath and through an arch which seemed almost a gothic entrance.

And stood transfixed in ecstasy.

Magnificent the dreams of man that took form in steel and stone and glass, yet none matched the lightness, the grace, the intricacy, the sublime simplicity of these interwoven crystalline structures where light from the noonday sun separated prismatically until it filled the air with myriads of living, darting, colored sparks of fire above him. Where the breeze that blew through the vibrating spires made blended sounds the ear could barely endure in rapture.

As once, in childhood, he had stood in a grove of giant trees that laced their limbs in gothic splendor above him, now again he stood, lost in time and space and being, lost in vision and in music which neither had nor needed form nor beginning nor end.

And knew it was a simple tool; Their concession to the mind of man, to bridge the gap between Their minds and his.

Without wondering more, he sank down upon the mossy turf of the floor and lay supine to gaze upward, to follow line to blended line until they seemed mirrored into infinity.

The darting lights above him whirled, spiraled up, then down, clockwise, then counterclockwise, reminding him . . . reminding him . . .

. . . the internal structure of crystals. . . .

25

Across the universe, two billion years ago, there too a planet coalesced from the mutually attracted vortices of twisted space; gases compelled by gravitational forces solidifying to hardened matter, forming a crust over a molten core. In the soupy atmosphere of metallic salts and gases, tortured and rent by electrical storms of incalculable fury, among the vibrating crystals one formed that was aware.

Not in the sharp awareness of later times, but at the first only ill-defined, perhaps no more than the awareness of acid chains of molecules that formed into non-crystalline viscid protoplasm on another planet across the universe. No distinct line of cleavage where affinity to other chemicals left off and sentient selectivity began marked the distinction here as in that protoplasm.

As with its cousin across the universe, the one-celled amoeba, these crystals too were sensitive to light, to heat, to cold—to food. Ill-defined, but distinct already from the non-sentient crystals about them, these life forms grew through absorbing from the rich and soupy atmosphere those elements necessary to growth, to branching, to cleavage into new individuals.

What is awareness? At what point even in protoplasmic life does it appear? The amoeba avoids pain, seeks food, reproduces itself, and blunders blindly through its environment in search for condition more favorable to its continuance.

In the monotony of a purposeless existence, most humans do no more than that.

Must awareness, too, be defined in terms of the consciousness of me-and-mine? Defined only by what me-and-mine can feel, know? A protoplasmic growth feeling awareness, excluding all possibility of awareness in other kinds of growth because they are not a part of me-and-mine, therefore too inferior to know awareness?

Each crystal structure has its own vibration characteristic, and on that planet, in time, one special vibratory rate knew awareness of self. Mutation here too gave added complexity to the structure, and self-awareness took on that added growth of awareness of surroundings.

Through eons of time, and the mutations brought by time, awareness of self and surroundings grew into awareness of wider peripheries, to sensing their world, its structure, its nature.

Another mutant leap and there was comprehension of other worlds, of other stars. Theirs was a vibratory awareness, directly akin to the vibrating fields of force which compose the material universe, and the vibrations of fields of force can be altered. To change their surroundings to a more suitable environment through vibration rates of things led surely to negation of distance. To change from crystal form to fields of energy and back again combined with negation of distance—they too spread out and out among the stars.

At first it was enough. But awareness is never still. Questions form.

In all the universe were they the only sentient thing? Did any cry but theirs rise to the stars, seeking to know? Because of the nature of their being their search was unconcerned with the outer shape of things which could be changed by them at will, but rather with the inner vibratory rate which would signal sentience, awareness.

They found no more than unconscious interaction of forces. Water runs down hill without knowing that it does, without the internal structure to provide the vibratory rate which would permit knowing.

For long eras they too were imprisoned within the confines of a me-and-mine envisioning, and it took a major leap for them to conceive that other structures than the crystalline might have a form of awareness. Alien to their kind, perhaps, yet a kind which must be acknowledged.

For they found something, at last, in a viscid non-crystalline substance, protoplasm.

On one distant planet this substance was already differentiated and specialized to a high degree. From the simplest to the most complex of its organization there were degrees of awareness, and in the most complex of these there was undeniable evidence of sentience outside of self.

Joy! Unparalleled ecstasy!

Recognition is not wisdom. With the unwisdom of inexperience in communicating with an unlike thing, not realizing that the values of their kind of awareness might not be the values of this differing kind, they rushed in with all their powers and forces, a joyful rapturous pyrotechnical display of material manipulation to show this new life form that they too were aware—to communicate that the loneliness of one might now be softened by the presence of the other.

And man fell down to the ground and groveled his face in the dust.

His awareness was of the outer shapes of things, his security lay in adapting himself to those shapes, his certainties lay in the dependability of those shapes. A rock was a rock.

But no! The crystals were delighted that they had brought something which they could share with this new life form. The rock could be a tree! See!

And lo, the rock was a tree.

And the people were sore afraid.

For that which had been certain and sure was no longer so.

This mountain wall which had formed an impassable barrier to migration into a new and richer valley was rent asunder, so! And beyond, the new valley beckoned. But the people huddled in their caves and dared not venture forth.

The vibrating entities, no longer dependent upon their crystalline forms, withdrew to confer among themselves. To one life form, awareness composed of the outer shape of things, the relationship of those shapes, security in the unchanging shape. To the other life form, awareness composed of the inner vibration, the relationships of those vibrations, with outer shapes changed at will, and therefore meaningless.

Yet even this protoplasmic life must see the changing shapes of things. The clouds that formed and disappeared; the seed that became root and stem and leaf and flower; the infant that became man, and man that decomposed as corpse. Surely this life form must see an inner cause! Surely they must see that even the permanent rock changed slowly into dust, that the eternal sea was restless, never still; that stars moved in the vault of heavens, warmth changed to cold and night to day. How did they account for changes in these outer forms if not by inner cause?

They changed the shapes of things themselves, these men; the seed ground into meal, the moving animal shot down with stick or stone and stilled and changed to food, the moving of the smaller rocks, erection of a dwelling made of poles and thatch to change environment for the man inside. Change, then, man knew; why fear the greater change, the easier one? Why tug and lift and strain to move the boulder from the path, when all was needed was to shift proportion in one tiny way, rebalance the equation of relationship with one slight thought, and lo, the stone no longer barred the way?

Too long ago, lost in the distant past, the crystals had forgot their own once-orientation of all other things to me-and-mine, forgot to credit it to man. To lift the boulder with one's strength to serve a purpose was within the ken of man, a thing that he could do. To see it lifted, moved, without his strength, bespoke a greater strength than his, and purpose that he could not understand. And man fell to his knees in fear and awe.

For man knew only one relation to all things—to conquer if he could, and force acknowledgment of superior strength and purpose. To kill if that acknowledgment was not given. To survive by giving that acknowledgment to a stronger one than he.

Man groveled in the dust, the only pattern of survival that he knew when strength beyond his own was shown. But even while he knelt, to scheme a way that he-and-his might find ascendancy in future days. The one invariable pattern persisting from the cave man dressed in furs to diplomat in striped pants, the only pattern possible while me-and-mine ascendant is the aim and goal.

To show another pattern then, the crystals aim. Ascendancy of me-and-mine was meaningless, belonged to orders of awareness lower than intelligence that they could meet in partnership. Instruct them, then. No joy or purpose in conquering them. No companionship in these disgusting grovelings. Show them the inner forces that controlled the outer shapes of things.

Once crystals, now divorced from hardened form, the outer shape of things was no longer a consideration in their life; but for this form of life, still dependent for that life upon the maintenance of material form, no doubt the shapes and forms of things were paramount to them. Well then, show them the true relationship, sketch out upon the sands the diagram of how the forces that control the shapes of things are interwoven, interact.

Before the kneeling men, the cabalistic diagrams took shape, and lo, a spring of water flowed from dry and barren stone.

But man saw only shape of diagram, its cabalistic lines and form. A sacred thing, a magic thing, a sign that he might draw with finger in the air or in the sand, protection from the evil forces that surrounded him.

The sentient fields of force withdrew. Too soon, too soon. Man was not ready for communication. Too soon, too soon.

But man did not forget, the memory lived on. And fathers spoke to sons, and made the outer forms of gestures, drew the cabalistic signs, and told of magic things and powers that these signs could do. To some, one diagram was shown, a way to build a house of stone that better weathered the storms of Earth. The house of stone became a holy place, a thing existing in its own right, and not, as was intended, an example of one use to which this arrangement of forces might be put.

And to some other man another diagram was shown, this time to slay an animal for food. And men fought wars over these differing symbols, each side determined to make its symbol ascendant over the other.

Deep within the Asian land where contact had been made, the memories lived on, and some of the meaning of the diagrams beyond their outer shape had gained way. The racial memory persisted, and in the latter Pleistocene epoch the knowledge of altering shapes through force of mind became a racial memory, coalesced into cults of belief, degenerated into forms and phrases; but from generation to generation the memory was kept alive that once, when the world was new, the form of things was indeed changed by thought. This holy man, far away and long ago, had pointed his finger at a tree, and lo! a beautiful nymph had stepped forth clad in jewels and coins to make him rich. This hero climbed a mountain and a voice spoke unto him, and proof of this were letters cut in stone. Well-witnessed, this divine one changed some water into wine, and fed a multitude from five small loaves and fishes.

A kind of radiation of its own, always the cults who sought the inner meanings formed within that Asian land and spread outward through the world.

But out on the periphery, and not exposed to thought of inner meanings, another cult took shape. Here concern was solely with the outer shape and size and weight and measurement of things, and how the size and shape and weight of one interacted with another. The Dravidian culture, which grasped only the idea but not the method of how the inner vibration could change the outer shape receded and became submerged in the Western cult that found a method in the measurement of shape and weight of things to make them change.

It was Rabindranath, centuries later, who described the essential difference between the Indian and the Grecian civilization as that between a forest culture which had known no walls, and a city culture where everything has limit and every inch must be mapped.

But perhaps, also, the Greeks had never seen this tree changed into bird, this cloud changed into flower. Not trapped by memories grown into tradition that must not die, they hit upon an approach that man could master. For it was the Greek beginnings which led to the Oxford definition of how to make scientific inquiry into the properties of things.

Inquiry into the properties, at first the outer shapes and weights, led inevitably straight back to vibrations. All matter is merely a specific vibration of energy, a range of vibrations feeling solid to the senses, as a range of light vibrations translate into color through the eyes.

$E = MC^2$!

It took man far. He too began an exploration of the stars!

Failure in their first attempt had brought a wisdom to the sentient fields of force. This time they did not rush in with pyrotechnic displays to show the wondrous power they knew. Observing patiently through the centuries, by now they knew man well. They knew his weakness, yet by making thing react with thing, he'd proved his strength. For here he was among the stars.

Perhaps by now he might communicate? Perhaps, by now, he would not prostrate himself and grovel in the dust, if someone said, "Hello!"

But careful, perhaps he would.

There had been a man by name of Galileo, with the first crude telescope he'd made, who first saw the rings of Saturn. But not as rings, but rather in the planet's tilting, he had seen a spot of light on either side. And sometime later, when he looked again, the tilting of the planet back had made the rings edge on, and so they disappeared. He never looked again, nor told of what he'd seen; for legend had it that the god Saturn periodically devoured his own children, and this phenomenon he'd seen, if it became widely known, would be interpreted as the proof the legend was correct—and do incalculable damage to scientific inquiry. He'd known the temper of his fellow man well enough to take no chances of this kind, to note the experience in his works, perhaps discuss it with a cautious friend or two, but to add no further fuel to the raging fires of superstition that consumed men's minds and seared out possibility of rational thought.

So walk with care. For superstition still is paramount, despite the fact that some men know how to reach the stars.

To communicate this time, the fields of force took a sere planet, of barren, blistered rock, and with a concept made it into the garden of man's dreams. On one island, they set up a crystalline structure, a thing, this much concession to the mind of man; a tool, to amplify and clarify their thought to reach the still rudimentary but nevertheless present centers of man's mind—some certain man who might be ready to receive that thought.

Placed in man's exploratory path, the waiting was not long until man found it. They had not led him to it through any intuitive change of course that he might find suspect. The explorers landed, claimed it for Earth, and went away. None among them felt any pull from the crystal tool upon the mountaintop.

The scientists came to make their measurements. Their busy minds were full of weight and size and the relationship of thing to thing. Perhaps by now they too were so committed to the use of a thing to act upon another thing that they could not countenance the thought that thought could act upon a thing direct. They measured the crystal tool, and recorded all their measurements, but found no meaning in its arches and its spires. If any felt the impact of the thinking of the fields of force, he made no sign nor gave response. Indeed, to preserve his status and reputation with his fellow scientists he'd not have dared admit a meaning that could not be measured with his instruments. Forevermore he'd be outcast, if he but hinted that he thought their science was insufficient to capture everything of meaning there. And to scientist most of all, his status with his fellow man means more than truth. At least to most. But are there some to whom the truth is paramount?

Yes, for had not scientist after scientist through the years risked and lost his status through his questioning? And then perhaps today there are such men.

So walk with care, and wait.

The colonists came, and as the scientists' minds had been filled with measurements and weights and analyses; the colonists' minds were filled with cabins, fields, food.

Surely, among men somewhere, there must be those not wholly captured on the one hand by formless superstition; and on the other hand not bound within the tightly narrowed circle of weight and measurement! Surely man must know by now he could not capture the inner meaning of a thing through a description of its outer surface.

But as long as man got by, and did great things by using physical things to act upon other physical things, even to considering the universal energy as a thing, he would look no farther.

All right then, a little nudge in another direction. Change the concept of the planet slightly, so that one thing cannot act upon another, no tool be used except this crystal set to act as intermediary. Let that happen, and out from Earth a man would come, perhaps a dozen men, perhaps a hundred ships, a thousand men, and all to find their ships, their tools, were gone. But someday there would come a man with mind trained in the ability to conceive that there might be a road to truth outside the useless superstitions that sent man to groveling in the dust at each small breath that blew, and also one who would not quit because he had no weather vane to test the direction of that breath.

And they would know when that mind came.

The first man came. Take away his tools and wait. He did not fall to earth in awe nor freeze in fear. His mind searched curiously. Enough. The man was here. Shield off the planet from the rest that he be undisturbed in his thought.

Could he go farther? Conceive the purpose of this lack of tools, that it was by design? And still not grovel in the dust? They'd made their move. Could he respond?

He drew a circle in the sand!

Joy! Ecstasy!

This time there might be surcease to the loneliness, and two intelligences so unlike commune. The very unlikeness of each bringing to the other thought not yet considered, and together going on to find . . . to find. . . .

Now let him see the fallacy of such strict measurement. Now let him think, to realize that measuring the balance of the status quo of things in only one relationship of an infinity of possibilities, to realize that he can change his measurements to balance an equation designed to express the status quo, or with equal truth, at his desire, he can change the status quo, the shape of things, to fit the equation he desires.

Let him wander, puzzled, worrying on this. Let him work it out himself, for experience from long ago had taught them that if man was not ready to accept an alien thought he could not, would not, accept but in his own interpreting.

Now, at last, at his readiness to make things fit the equation he conceives, instead of making the equation fit the things as they are, bring him closer in the range of the amplifier, the crystal tool, that communication might be direct.

He holds the key.

He knows the lock.

He finds the door.

Show him the one small step remaining—the diagram, the design, the movement of the forces of his mind.

To turn the key.

Unlock the lock.

Throw wide the door.

26

As one awakened from a deep sleep, a hypnotic trance, Cal opened his eyes.

Man's ancient thought filled his being, the subject of man's dreams, of yearnings, of philosophies. In ancient eidetic memory, the unbroken thread persisted: If I could only grasp this elusive thing, always just barely beyond my reach, I would not need the ox, the wagon, the train, the plane, the spaceship to transport me from here to there.

And now, at last, the thought was in Cal's grasp. Express the things and forces balanced in equation to describe them as they are; or, equally, to alter the things and forces instead to fit the equation balance one had in mind; purely a matter of choice. Each was the use of natural law. No chaos here, no magic, one as much true science as the other.

How long had he slept, and dreamed? A few minutes? An hour? Or by chance was he another Rip Van Winkle, doomed to find the colonists aged or dead?

But why wonder?

A short distance first, just outside the amphitheater, just a small test. He first rearranged the relative position of himself to the amphitheater, to be outside instead of in it. He diagrammed the forces in his mind that would alter the relationship, connected them.

He was standing outside the entrance arch.

With a hoarse cry, Louie, who had been watching all the while through the open arch, shrank back away from Cal, wavered in uncertainty, then fell to his knees, then groveled in the dust.

"Forgive me!" he cried. "In my blind, senseless vanity, I did not know you were a Holy One. I was going to kill you, I confess. Woe! Woe! I saw you lying there in Their temple, defaming it in blasphemy by your sleep. But when I tried to enter, I could not. Their will prevented me. Some shielding force protected you. And then I knew you were a Holy One. Forgive me. Let me live to expiate my sin."

"Louie, Louie," Cal said sadly.

As if in tangled ball, the thought stream of Louie, twisted and warped by the false reasonings and interpretations fed to him in childhood, seemed clearly revealed to Cal. Again a change in concept of relationship to reality, the schematic of forces visualized, the untangling, straightening of thought.

Louie scrambled to his feet, a rueful grin on his face.

"Sorry, Cal," he said. "I must have gone nuts there for a while, shock and all. I'm all right now. Don't worry anymore about me. I'll get on back to the rest."

"Sure, Louie. See you there," Cal agreed.

A rearrangement of relationships, and Cal walked out from behind a bush to approach Jed and Tom.

"You must not have gone all the way to the top," Jed said when he looked up and caught sight of Cal. "It's just barely past noon, I reckon. Didn't expect to see you back until nightfall."

"I took a short cut," Cal said with a grin. "Little past noon," he continued, as if musing with a thought. "About the same time of day that everything happened a couple of weeks ago."

"Yeah, about the same time of day," Jed said, and looked at him curiously.

Tom had arisen to his feet and was staring at Cal curiously, sensing a difference in the E. Now Jed felt it too, and looked at Cal with puzzlement on his face.

"There's something important about it being around this time of day, Cal?" he asked.

"Not really," Cal said, "but I thought it might be helpful. I could restore the village, the fields, the escape ship, everything just as it was; make it feel like a continuation of the same day to the people. It being the same time of day would help the illusion that no time had passed, nothing had happened."

Tom's eyes narrowed in speculation.

"You can do that, Cal?" he asked. "You've solved the problem?"

"Yes," Cal said simply. "I'll tell you about it sometime. There's quite a few loose ends to catch up right now." He turned to Jed. "How about it, Jed?" he asked. "Think it'll be too much of a shock to put things back as they were?"

In spite of himself, Jed was trembling. He drew a deep breath, firmed his jaw. Seemed to set himself as one does in the dentist's chair at the approach of the drill.

It was a bigger equation, a more complex one, but not different in kind.

The village of Appletree sprang suddenly into being, the hangar with the metallic gleam of the ship inside, the fields, the pasture fences with the calves separated from the cows. A few people, clothed, were walking on the dirt street between the houses. They looked at one another. They looked up at the sky, at the fields around them, the forests beyond. They looked back at one another. They shook their heads, and blinked their eyes, as if suddenly wakened from a sleep, a dream, the craziest dream.

Later they would compare the dream, and with Jed's help piece together, and feel the shock, and wonder.

Upon the hill, away from the village, where Jed lay, clothed, in the hammock swung between two trees, Martha came out of the house, clothed.

"I must have sat down in a chair for a minute and fallen asleep or something, Jed," she said as she came to stand beside him. "And I had the funniest dream. You can't imagine. You know how

173

sometimes we'll dream about being out in front of folks, all naked. . . ."

"That wasn't any dream, Martha," he answered with a grin. "All the people in the village are going to start realizing it pretty soon. They'll need some help. We'd better walk down there. Them people across the ridge, too. Bet they'll be hightailing it back over here first thing you know. And something else, there's an E ship here, come to find out why we didn't communicate."

"Well whatever on Earth are you talkin' about, Jed?" she asked curiously. "It won't be time to communicate for a couple of days yet. You ought to know that. Have you been dreaming, too? Or you and the boys fermenting something? Here, let me smell your breath!"

"Aw, now Martha," he said with a huge grin. He clambered out of the hammock and stood up, took her in his arms, hugged her tightly.

"Jed!" she scolded. "Right out here in the front yard in front of everybody." But she didn't struggle away from him.

"Won't matter a bit," he said. "Not after what's been goin' on in front of everybody right along."

"Whatever has been goin' on can't be half as bad as what I've been dreamin'," she said.

"Better start gettin' used to the idea that it wasn't a dream, Martha," he cautioned.

"Jed!" she scolded again, her face aflame with embarrassment.

27

The communications operator looked up as the supervisor came down the aisle toward him.

"Communication from the E.H.Q. ship at Eden coming in just fine," he said enthusiastically. He'd thought it over and decided he'd better repair some fences. Good job here, no use letting his irritation with the supervisor's old-maid fussiness make him cut off his nose to spite his face.

"See that it does," the supervisor answered sharply. He recognized the overture for what it was, felt relieved that he wouldn't have any more insubordination, was willing to let bygones be bygones—after a suitable period of punishment. "What's been happening?" he asked with a curiosity that got the better of his desire to discipline.

"E Gray has come back out of that quartz outcropping where we lost him. He's standing there talking to the astronavigator who followed him up the mountain."

"More of the same, I guess," the supervisor said. "Nothing's happened for ten days. Nothing likely to happen," he said. He turned and started back down the aisle toward his own office.

"Wait a minute," the operator called. "Here's something."

Other operator heads raised up all down the aisle.

"Now, now; now, now!" the supervisor quarreled at them. "Get on with your work, nothing to concern you here, none of your business."

But of course it was everybody's business. Anything different was everybody's business. All over the world everybody was wondering about the enigma of Eden, everybody speculating, everybody with a different answer. Some were gleeful that science had finally got its comeuppance, and felt no more than a pleasure that the bigdomes had proved they weren't any smarter than anybody else. Others took an equal pleasure in crying woe, woe, at this proof there were mysteries beyond man's knowing, woe, woe, now that man would be punished for trying to know what he was not meant to know.

The operator took time out, in spite of the supervisor's admonishments, to listen frankly.

"They've lost sight of the E," the operator exclaimed. "No, wait a minute. There he is, down in the valley, coming out from behind a bush to talk to the pilot and the head man of the colony."

"Can't have happened like that," the supervisor grumbled. "Ten or twelve miles from that mountain top to the valley. The ship has garbled their reporting. Probably got behind in reporting and then just decided to skip the journey back, and pick up to make it current. There's going to be complaints about this."

"Well, you were right here," the operator said. "You were listening. I didn't skip anything. It wasn't my fault."

"All right, all right."

"Wait a minute," the operator said. "Here, listen in."

The supervisor's eyes grew round.

"Can't be," he exclaimed.

"All the buildings, everything's just like it was before," the operator said loudly to the room at large. "All of a sudden, the way they report it."

"They're faking the reports," the supervisor grumbled irritably. "Have to be."

"Now, no matter how much they fake, you can't rebuild all those buildings in a couple hours," the operator argued.

"None of our business," the supervisor cautioned. "We just take the reports. Can't criticize us for whatever the E.H.Q. ship out there's doing."

"And everybody's got their clothes back on," the operator said loudly.

There was a sigh of regret up and down the aisle.

"Now the E's disappeared again," the operator said. "They're scanning all over, trying to find him."

The supervisor put down his headset with resolution.

"I'm going to my office to make a report on the sloppy way this reporting has been done. There's going to be fur flying over these skips and jumps, and I don't want it to be our fur. Best thing is to make the complaint first," he said to the room at large. "Now you call me if there's any more of this bollux," he said to the operator as he left.

An hour passed while the supervisor sat in his office. He wrote furiously, scratched out, wrote some more, tore up papers and threw them in the vague direction of the wastebasket, started afresh to write some more. How to report without stepping on anybody's toes?

His buzzer sounded softly to give him respite, and he looked up from a virtually blank piece of paper to the board. The Eden operator again.

"Oh, no," he groaned. But he left his desk at once and half trotted up the aisle.

"Now the captain of the ship says he wants Sector Chief Hayes at once," the operator called out. "Something very important."

"Very well," the supervisor said. "Ring him."

But Hayes didn't wait for the ring. He had been listening, red eyed, tired, gaunt for lack of sleep.

"Give me connection," he said to the operator as soon as the line opened.

"Bill Hayes here, Captain," he said, as soon as he received the signal. "What now?"

"Mrs. Gray, the Junior E's wife, has disappeared from aboard ship," the Captain said without any preliminaries.

"What do you mean 'disappeared'?" Hayes asked. "How could she disappear in deep space? Have you looked everywhere? Checked the lifeboats? Maybe she took one and tried to get down to her husband by herself."

"We've looked everywhere. No lifeboats missing. No port has opened. You ought to know we wouldn't bother you until we'd checked everything out first."

"She can't have disappeared into thin air, thin space," Hayes quarreled back. "She must be on your ship somewhere. When was she last seen?"

"That's—ah—that's mainly why I'm calling you, Bill," the captain said. "A wild tale, obviously a mistake. One of the crewmen passed her stateroom about an hour ago. Door was open and he looked in, the way anybody does. Says he saw her standing inside her cabin embracing a man. Says he didn't stop to look close, but he was pretty sure it was E Gray. Says he knows because he's had access to the viewscope and has watched E Gray on the surface of Eden."

"There's been no report of any ship leaving Eden, joining you, Captain," Hayes said accusingly.

"Because there hasn't been any," the captain snapped back. "So it can't have been E Gray she was embracing. That's why I called you. Looks like we're going to have some petty scandal mixed up with everything else."

"Looks like it, then," Hayes said with a vast weariness. "Some member of your crew, or one of the scientists," he said. "Keep looking. Somebody's hiding her, probably to keep the scandal from breaking. But it seems odd to me that she was so anxious to get out there near her husband and then in ten days she'd. . . ."

"Maybe her real anxiety was to be near somebody already assigned to the ship," the captain said. "I mean, we've got to consider all the possibilities. Somebody she knew there at E.H.Q."

"Keep checking, Captain. I'll see if the Board wants to contact

E McGinnis. Maybe he knows what's been going on around here that could lead us to the guy who's hiding her."

"I'll keep checking, but she's not on board *my* ship," the captain said. He sighed. Bill Hayes sighed. They broke connection.

Hayes made contact with the Board chairman. It took only a few minutes to spin the latest tale of woe. Another minute for the Board to decide direct intervention.

"Now they want me to make contact with the other ship," the operator said to the supervisor. "The Wheel himself wants to know if E McGinnis will talk to him."

"Well, contact it, contact it," the supervisor commanded urgently.

"I'm doing it! I'm doing it!" the operator quarreled back.

The both of them listened in on the conversation, on the grounds that testing the quality of reception was a necessity. E McGinnis's pilot was quite explicit.

"E McGinnis left orders that under no circumstances was he to be disturbed," the pilot said. "He, E Gray and Mrs. Gray are in his cabin, in conference."

"E Gray! Mrs. Gray!" the chairman exploded. "Impossible. How the devil did they get into your ship?"

"Don't ask me," the pilot said in a tired voice. "I just work here. I'm sitting here minding my own business. I see E McGinnis's door open. He leans out the door and gives me my orders. I look past him and I see E Gray and Mrs. Gray sitting in the room. Don't ask me how they got in there. I don't know. But I do know this, I'm going to get myself a nice quiet milk run to Saturn or someplace, soon as I get back to E.H.Q. If I ever do get back."

"Now, now," the Board chairman soothed. "I'm sure there's a simple explanation." Crewmen willing to pilot an E around the universe were hard to find.

"Yeah? After what I've seen out here, I don't think I'd even want to hear it," the pilot said, and without apology cut off the communication.

28

Had the pilot been able, a moment later, to look into the E's stateroom he would have seen still another visitor, another who had not entered his ship by any normal means.

Attorney General Gunderson sat in a chair facing the two E's and Linda. He seemed stunned, frozen into immobility. Only his eyes were alive, darting here and there, unbelieving. There is limit to the number of shocks the mind can withstand, and the series had come too fast for him to adjust to them.

He too had picked up Junior E Gray as soon as he came through the arch of the quartz outcropping on top of the mountain, the structure that somehow interfered with their visoscope's ability to penetrate and see what went on inside. He had been watching when Gray suddenly disappeared from where he had been talking with the astronavigator. That had been a shock, immediately followed by a greater one, when the ship's operator had scanned the valley and found Gray talking with the E's pilot and the chief of the colonists. There was no way in which the journey could have been made that rapidly.

He was still watching when the village, the fields, the escape ship, the E ship all had suddenly materialized before his eyes. And the people were all clothed. It couldn't be done, but he had seen it. But he kept his head. E science must be farther along than he'd realized, to produce a miracle such as this—but it was science. He must hold to that, otherwise. . . .

He saw his case begin to melt out from under him, and he made one more effort to regain some measure of control. He gave his own pilot orders to land on the surface of Eden. He transmitted orders to the other two police ships to follow in close formation; the three of them to land and take custody.

But the barrier still remained, and the ships could not penetrate it.

He told himself that all wasn't lost. Maybe the E was back in control of Eden, but he, Gunderson, still had a morals case. All those photographs! Some of the press and commentators might desert him, now that the Junior had proved adequate to the job. Unless he chose carefully, some stupid judge might decide the means were justified by the end result. But there were those photographs, and the world was full of Mrs. Grundy. He might have to back up a little bit on the incompetence of the Junior E, but Mrs. Grundy would be behind him a hundred per cent on the morals issue—when he released some of the photographs, and titillated her nasty imagination by reference to others too indecent to release.

It was then that the observer ship got a call through to him, and told him that the photographs, every one of them, had disappeared from the ship's vault where they had been locked, and the only thing remaining in the vault was one little slip of paper which read, "Shame on you for taking feelthy pictures. Naughty, naughty! Calvin Gray."

The case was crumbling, but all was not lost. He still had witnesses. He thought for a minute and began to wonder about those witnesses. Any judge, anybody around the courts, anybody connected with the press, and maybe even some of the public knew that any police officer will swear to any lie to back up another police officer because he might need the favor returned tomorrow.

Without concrete evidence. . . .

He suddenly found himself standing in the cabin of the E ship, confronted by E McGinnis, Junior E Gray, and Mrs. Gray. He sank down in a chair and sat frozen, immobile. Only his eyes were alive, darting frantically here and there as if expecting some hole to open up and swallow him—perhaps wishing one would.

"I don't know just what to do with you," Cal said a little sadly, ruefully. "Far as the E's are concerned, you've only been a minor nuisance, hardly worth noticing, but your intentions were dangerous. As far back as man's history goes the growth of police powers immediately preceded and caused the fall and destruction of each culture.

"It is a law of the nature of man that he will resist the ascendancy of any special me-and-mine group over him; that this resistance will grow until man will even destroy himself in the attempt to destroy that ascendancy. In more recent history it was the growth, extension, and severity of the police in controlling every activity of man that destroyed both the United States and Russia.

"Now you are attempting to rebuild that same police control in world government. The result will be the same. Man will destroy himself in trying to destroy you.

"We in E don't want that to happen. We see no need of it. We have already warned that the attitude of the police toward the public is the major cause of crime, that crime will increase with each increase of police power and severity until the whole structure rots and crumbles.

"Yet man has not yet progressed far enough to know how to maintain an organized society without some special body to enforce that organization. It's a problem which the E's haven't solved, probably because we know too little about the natural laws affecting the behavior of man. Perhaps it is still a field belonging to non-science, because science doesn't know enough yet to take hold of it.

"I would suggest, Gunderson, that you turn your talents and

your organization to solving this problem of how to build an organized society instead of destroying it."

The chair where Gunderson had sat was empty.

E McGinnis looked at Cal; he too was sitting silent and immobile. But E science had innured him to shock. He waited because it was E Gray's show, and he was letting Cal handle it.

"Where is he now?" McGinnis asked when he saw the empty chair.

"Sitting at his desk in his office back on Earth," Cal said with a grin. "Our boy has a few things to think about."

"You've explained the theory back of all this"—McGinnis changed the subject—"but I still find it incredible. It's still just theory."

"Well," Cal said, "theory comes first. Even to add two and two, you first have to get the idea that it can be done, a theory of how it is done, but that still won't get you four. You've got to learn how to apply the theory.

"When I first found I knew how, I was pretty concerned. The whole basis of science is that anybody can do it, anybody who follows the step-by-step method. It doesn't take any special gifts that can't be trained. I had visions of a world, a universe of people, in possession of this theory and method before they were wise enough to use it, and chaos.

"But when I thought it over, I stopped worrying. The methods of science are also open to all. But few bother to learn them. Most prefer their frustrations and their miseries to making the effort which will solve them. For centuries the libraries containing all the accumulated knowledge and wisdom of mankind have been free and open to anybody who wants to read, but few have bothered to absorb that knowledge and that wisdom.

"This new key we have that unlocks the door to another vista of knowledge, another point of view whereby we can change material things to suit our desire, is merely another advance of science. For science, after all, is no more than organized knowledge of reality. You can't multiply six times six until you've learned how to add two and two. Most people won't bother.

"It will be a long, long time before any significant number will graduate through all the normal seven steps of E science to become ready for the eighth. Some of the E's will master it, but you know how few E's there are. And the E's have enough restraint, wisdom, and selflessness to use this new knowledge for the benefit of man instead of his detriment.

"I suspect that one has to be graduated beyond the desire to make me-and-mine ascendant over others before he can absorb this knowledge."

"Maybe that's my trouble," McGinnis said slowly. "I've been thinking, all along, of how much power this gives the E's. Wondering if even the E's should have that much power over others."

Linda spoke up.

"E McGinnis," she said, "Cal has solved the problem of what happened to the colonists, why they didn't communicate. Do you thing this will qualify him for his big E?"

Both men burst into laughter.

"No question of it, Linda," E McGinnis said with a chuckle. "But I doubt it really matters to E Gray, now. He can do things none of the rest of us can do, and the real question now is whether we have the right to call ourselves Seniors until we can match his ability."

"I think," Cal said slowly, "we'd better recommend to E.H.Q. that the colonists be withdrawn from Eden, assigned somewhere else. I've left the shield around the planet so none can enter or leave without the eighth key. I can unlock the door and close it again. Perhaps Eden should become the next step for the E, the next hurdle he must cross.

"When I've sent my ship and crew back to Earth, and we've removed all the colonists, it might be a good idea to restore Eden to what it was when I arrived—a place where no tools will work, no physical tools. To qualify for E, a man will be put on the island, where he can live as we lived, to work out the step-by-step method. When he's ready, he can go into the thought-amplifier on top of the mountain, and if his mind is open enough to the potentials he'll receive the final step of instruction—as I did.

"One by one, as the E's shake free of their present projects, they can take this next step."

"I'm not working on any project right now," E McGinnis said hopefully.

"I'll be right back," Cal said with a grin, "and we'll get started on it."

The chair where he had been sitting was empty.

29

Cal stood within the crystal amphitheater atop the mountain and watched the interplay of lights until he felt communion come.

Rapture! Joy!

Question?

"Be patient," he said. "There will be more, and more, and more. "You had an advantage," he reminded Them. "You started with a crystalline vibration nearer to the force field than that possible in protoplasm. We've had to come up the hard way.

"But we have come up.

"You had no competition. We've had to fight for our very lives every inch of the way, endure the setbacks lasting for centuries, millennia. It is no wonder that the me-and-mine-ascendant concept has dominated all our thought, and does still. Without it, we'd not have survived at all.

"It takes time to outgrow it, to learn we can survive without it. Five hundred years after Copernicus, a survey of the high school students in the United States revealed that a third of them still rejected his knowledge, still believed the Earth to be at the center of the universe and man was the reason why the universe had been created at all. But two thirds had adjusted.

"More important, there *was* a Copernicus.

"Don't sell man short because he's slow to learn, and you are impatient for fuller, deeper exploration of the truths in reality. He has much to offer you, as you to him. Competition for survival has given him ingenuity.

"Once all learned men believed the Earth to be the center of the universe, but there *was* a Copernicus who asked the question, 'What if it isn't so?'

"Millions of men watched apples fall to the ground, but one *did* ask if this might not be the key to the structure of the universe, the balance of the stars.

"Billions watched the stars, but finally one *did* ask, 'What if the light be curved instead of straight?'

"There is capacity in man, this protoplasmic life, that had to learn an ingenuity which might surpass even yours.

"This is not the final door in the corridor of thought. Still other doors, on down the corridor, are yet to be explored. And you may need these special gifts of man to open them, as he has needed this new room of thought.

"Be patient. A million or a billion may come here to seek the method that can change things to fit the equation of desire, before one comes who asks a question even you have not conceived.

"But someday he *will* come—and ask."

The lights danced faster now in patterns of delight.

www.ingramcontent.com/pod-product-compliance
Lightning Source LLC
Chambersburg PA
CBHW030336180626
46810CB00003B/1385